Sheikh Jassim Al-Thani
Founder of Qatar

A HISTORICAL STUDY OF A NINETEENTH-CENTURY GULF AND THE ARABIAN PENINSULA

7.3.2018

DR. OMAR AL-EJLI

TRANSLATED BY
PROFESSOR ABDUL SALAM IDRISI

PAGE PUBLISHING, INC.
New York, NY

First originally published by Page Publishing, Inc. 2015

ISBN 978-1-68213-325-5 (pbk)
ISBN 978-1-68213-326-2 (digital)

Printed in the United States of America

Sheik Yasim ben Mohammed ben Thoni; Sheik de Katar 1882

This drawing of Sheikh Jassim Al-Thani drawn by a French traveler in 1882. It was inherited by his son Sheikh Fahd. The author Dr. Omar El-Ejli received it personally from sheikh Saud bin Fahd, the grand son of Sheikh Jassim Al-Thani.

PREFACE

Since I lived in Qatar, I became interested in reading about the history of this Emirates. I came across Sheikh Jassim bin Mohammed Al-Thani quite often as being the founder of Qatar, as an independent political entity. I think that any person who reads what renowned historians, nineteenth- and twentieth-century dignitaries, and officials wrote about Sheikh Jassim will wonder what kind of a person he was to be appraised by his foes as his friends did. I, therefore, found myself searching for sources and documents about Sheikh Jassim and Qatar. This search led me to go further in the history of the Arab Gulf and the Arabian Peninsula as they are closely related to what happened in Qatar.

It became unequivocal to me that Sheikh Jassim was the most outstanding political leader of his era in the Arab Gulf and the eastern region of the Arabian Peninsula. His influence went much further than his country and neighboring areas to reach the Ottoman Sultan. As it is shown in the book, Sheikh Jassim single-handedly unified tribes that were fighting for trivial matters and had them pledge allegiance to his leadership.

The reader will find Sheikh Jassim a true Muslim in his manners—generous to the poor, helping the aggressed, kind to all people, just in making judgment, etc. He was in front of his army in the battlefield. He was blessed by God with instant thinking and sound mind. Just to cite an example, who would resign his post as the ruler of Qatar after he was victorious in the Al-Wejba battle?

Although Sheikh Jassim was the center of this study, it gives the reader the history of the Arab Gulf and Arabian Peninsula as well as some hints on the Ottoman Empire and the role of the British in the region. We, therefore, tried to dig in deeply through the documents in Turkey about the history of the era before the emergence of Sheikh Jassim and during his long life, not only about Qatar but also the entire region. I visited Istanbul, Turkey, three times for that purpose. I got hold of several British documents as well as books and articles on the subject.

The book is divided into eight chapters. The first one gives a perspective of the subject, our goals of writing the book, and the limitation of this endeavor. I tried to throw light on the life of this charismatic personality of the nineteenth and early twentieth centuries.

The second chapter provides geographical, historical, and economic information to the reader to understand the following chapters.

Chapter 3 introduces the reader to the history of the Arab Gulf region before the emergence of Sheikh Jassim leadership. It also includes the newly awakened Ottoman Empire and its struggle with its competing rivalries in the region: the Dutch, the Portuguese, the British, and the Persians.

Chapter 4 describes the political status quo of the region prior to Midhat Pasha's campaign. It shows the Ottoman Empire revived from its longtime slumber, during which it neglected its possessions in the Arab Gulf and Arabian Peninsula. The new reformers tried to regain the Ottomans' dignity and control of the region.

Chapter 5 covers the details of Midhat Pasha's campaign, including its administrative and military plans. It goes into the field combats of liberating cities of Nejd, Al-Ahsa'a, and other Eastern region of Arabian Peninsula.

Chapter 6 elaborates on the political environment in which Sheikh Jassim leadership emerged. Qatar was annexed to the Ottoman Empire with Sheikh Jassim being its administrator. This arrangement was part of the administrative reform of the regional troops.

Chapter 7 gives a description of Al-Wejba Battle or what the Ottoman sultan called it, Qatar incident. The battle was designed by the Governor of Basra, Hafidh Pasha, to get rid of Sheikh Jassim and install a Turkish administrator in Qatar. But the result was victory for Sheikh Jassim and his troops, the escape of Hafidh Pasha to Bahrain, and the independence of Qatar. The chapter also provides several views on the battle, its reasons, its field operations, and its political and military consequences.

The final chapter covers events during Sheikh Jassim's rule and his style of government. It also shows how he became a renowned leader in the region. Qatar, under his guidance, became fully independent.

* * *

CHAPTER 1

GENERAL VIEW

INTRODUCTION

Before the reader starts reading this book, I have to tell him or her that the name, attributes, and news of Sheikh Jassim bin Mohammed Al-Thani are repeated so many times throughout the book. I would like to have the reader look at this charismatic personality from many angles to understand how he accomplished what seemed to be mission impossible. He became the property of history as all great leaders in the future are destined.

There have been thousands of chiefs of tribes or community leaders who came and left without being noted by historians or researchers. But Sheikh Jassim was able to bring together scattered tribes often fighting with each other to unite them under his leadership. He led his fellow tribesmen toward an independent country. What distinguished Sheikh Jassim's accomplishment from that of other local leaders was he did not solicit foreign power for assistance. Hence, Qatar's independence was a pure one.

Our methodology is to avoid going into details of events, especially if they had no great bearing on the personality of Sheikh Jassim and/or Qatar. There are many sources that go into details of those events. Our interest is to look at this unique person from different angles before his leadership and during his reign in Qatar.

We realized that with his sharp mind and the ability to foresee the future, Sheikh Jassim was able to guide his ship through the waves of events in the middle of great foreign powers' struggle for the region. He was raised by his father, who was a chief of tribe of great caliber. Above all, Sheikh Jassim was guided by God as he was a strong believer in the Creator and his pure religion. He was never an arrogant person or a dictator. He always used to seek advice from other chiefs and elderly people. He followed Prophet Mohammed's advice of seeking God's guidance before taking any decision.

His decision to invite the Ottoman troops to Qatar after being in the eastern region of the Arabian Peninsula had multipurpose goals: to avoid having the troops invade Qatar as they did in Nejd and Al-Ahsa'a, to prevent the British from invading Qatar claiming that they wanted to protect it, and to show that Sheikh Jassim was a friend of the Ottomans. This was considered by the Ottoman Sultan as a good gesture from Sheikh Jassim.

Sheikh Jassim was very clever in his maneuvering with the British to escape their inducements sometimes and threats at others. However, the British used the expulsion Indian merchants (the Banyans) from Qatar as an excuse to threaten Sheikh Jassim. The British were backed and encouraged by the Persians. But Sheikh Jassim stood firm and used his political shrewdness to prevent the British from attacking Qatar. This incident raised him from a chief of tribe to become a renowned leader in the region.

Sheikh Jassim was smart in dealing with the Ottoman governors to earn their respect rather than have them marginalize him as a low-ranking administrator subordinate. He took a lesson from what happened to Rashid bin Mghamis and his brother Mana'a, who surrendered the Basra governorate to the Ottomans. The latter kicked the two brothers out and appointed a Turkish governor. Sheikh Jassim realized that the governors of Basra tried to minimize the importance of Qatar as they did with Qatif and Haffoof.

When the Ottoman chief administrative of Nejd, A'akif Pasha, designed a program in collaboration with the British authority in

Bahrain to get rid of Sheikh Jassim, the latter acted in a shrewd way ahead of the collaborators by resigning his post as the administrator of Qatar. Hence, he created a political vacuum. He showed the Ottomans how important he was. They realized that Qatar would be in chaos without him. Besides, he became more respected by all parties, local and foreign.

Sheikh Jassim realized that the military campaign initiated by the governor of Basra, Hafidh Pasha, was to eliminate him as encouraged by the British. The latter came to a conclusion that Sheikh Jassim stood as a barrier against their advance into the western coast of the Gulf. Sheikh Jassim prepared his people and took Al-Wejba Castile as the protector of his troops. His victory became the main subject of gatherings in the Ottoman capital and the governors. Consequently, instead of being destroyed by the governor of Basra, his status was elevated in the eyes of everybody, including the Sultan, while the governor was fired from his post.

When the British conspired with some Ottoman officials in Nejd to defeat Sheikh Jassim, who stood against their infiltration into the region for two decades, he turned the table around and defeated those traders. He went further by saving their captured troops, treating them as his guest. Yet their army officers deserted them by fleeing to British ships and Bahrain. In order to protect himself from those officers who could lie to higher authorities, he dispatched a letter to his close friend Mohammed Sa'eed, the chief of the nobles of Basra, explaining the event, the conspiracy behind it, and its outcome. Therefore, he covered himself militarily and politically.

Since he had to fight the invading Ottoman troops in Al-Wejba battle and became victorious, he had to show that he was compelled to fight. He played it very smart by submitting his resignation from his post as Qatar district administrator. By doing so, he influenced the Enquiry Committee sent for fact-finding regarding the incident. The committee members thought that Sheikh Jassim was not fighting for his position because he had resigned. Besides, with his resignation, he calmed down the Sultan, who was furious about the defeat of his troops. The Sultan began to think that it was not Sheikh Jassim to blame for the incident. Sheikh Jassim showed his loyalty to the Sultan. The following is a summary of the resignation:

> To his Excellence the Amir of the Muslims the Caliph Sultan Abdul Hammed. I served your esteemed Government for 24 years since I was 40 years old. I am now at the age of 65. I had vast wealth from trade and pearls that I spent a great deal of during my service of your respected Government. I had not received a Para or a Rupee for my administrative work. Now my youth and wealth have gone. Since I do not have the strength or the money to run the District of Qatar, I shall be grateful to God then to the Amir if I would be relieved from my post while staying in full loyalty to you. I sent similar letter to the Governor of Basra, Hamdi Pasha. Please accept my greetings.

(16 Muharam 1310 Hijri, 1 July 1893)

With his resignation, Sheikh Jassim showed his desire to leave the spotlight even for some time. He also showed his willingness to cooperate with the Enquiry Committee. He used his cleverness when the British tried to attack then occupy Al-Zibara and Al-A'adid. The British wanted to put foot in the north and south of Qatar by taking over these two localities. Sheikh Jassim realized the plan of the British. He hastened to rally all the tribes behind him to defend these localities, preventing the British from being anywhere on the western shores of the Gulf. He considered this task as important as defending Qatar itself.

He was considered a regional leader when he led his army to restore the right of Mohammed Al-Sabah's sons after their father had been assassinated. His move created great debate among politicians in Istanbul, Basra, and Baghdad as well as British authorities in Bushier and Bahrain. Whatever the intention was, Sheikh Jassim was looked at as a regional leader who would not allow injustice to happen in the Gulf region. Besides, political powers began to expect that Sheikh Jassim might be incited to expand his territory beyond Qatar.

Finally, his plan, strategy, and influence within Qatar and surrounding areas led to his accomplishment of full independence of Qatar without the assistance of foreign powers. Sheikh Jassim anticipated the downfall of the Ottoman Empire. Hence, he avoided having Qatar still being part of it when this happened. That is why Qatar was not included in partitioning of the Ottoman Empire after World War I by the Allied Forces as what happened to Bin Rasheed of the Arabian Peninsula.

SHEIKH JASSIM AND THE IMPORTANCE OF WRITING ABOUT HIM

The historian may hesitate to write, though he is capable; the literary man may not find the words to describe; and the mind may wonder how to explore such a personality that is well rounded as an outstanding picturesque painting. He is like a dining table that contains a delicious variety of food that satisfies the historian, the literary man, the politician, and the student. Allah has created outstanding men and women to guide their fellow people for generations, just like a lighthouse does for ships.

We are here facing a man of such an excellent caliber that filled the vacuum of his era. He is Sheikh Jassim bin Mohammed Al-Thani. The best description to his heart that he liked to be characterized with is being adherent to Islam. He was a descendent of a religious family. All tribes of Qatar delegated him the authority of being their chief, spokesman, and decision maker. Usually, we find in other Arab areas two forms: tribes remain independent of each other to the extent of even fighting for trivial matters, or one tribe is strong enough to overcome by force or threat to surrender to the strong one. But in the case of Qatar, the tribes voluntarily selected Sheikh Jassim as the chief of their alliance. They found him a strong man, forbearing, independent in decision making, generous, and dignified. His huge wealth allowed him to be a giver and not a receiver. He had never accepted a salary for his post as an administrator of Qatar from the Ottoman Empire.

We believe that his character, manners, and courage in taking decisions were influenced by his adherence to the pure religion of Islam away from any innovation or invention. He believed in Islam as it is prescribed in the Quran and the authentic tradition of Prophet Mohammed (PBUH). He never feared anyone but Allah (God), and he followed the Prophet's saying, that no one could harm him except by Decree of Allah. From such belief, his courage came. It is known in Islam that such people, Allah protects them and guides to take the right decisions. He never accepted any gift or promise of reward from a foreign power. He was not getting a salary from the Ottoman Empire was included.

Sheikh Jassim was a descendant of a noble family that belonged to a reputable tribe, Beni Tamim. His family was known to be religious, well mannered, generous, and always rushed to help the needy. His tribe was recognized for breeding great knights, famous poets, and renowned Islamic jurisprudents. Just to name few—Al-Ahnaf; the well-known poets Jareer and Al-Farazdaq; and the founder of the Wahhabi tradition, Mohammed bin Abdul Wahhab. No wonder that Sheikh Jassim had them all from his ancestors: poetry, religion, good manners, generosity, and bravery.

Abu Huraira, one of the Prophet's companions, narrated that Prophet Mohammed (PBUH) described bani Tamim as saying "They will be the hardest on the False Masaya [anti-Christ]; when their alms came, he said these alms are from my people; and told his wife A'aisha to free her she slave, who was from bani Tamim, for she is a descendent of Prophet Ismail."

After the death of Mohammed bin Abdul Wahhab, who was from the Ma'adhid, a branch of bani Tamim, another star came up of that tribe, namely, Sheikh Jassim. If we compared him with other tribal sheikhs of the Gulf and Arabian Peninsula, we would find him with stronger personality, more popular among his people, greatly admired by his friends and foes, and having never solicited foreign assistance, just to mention a few things.

Therefore, he was the man of the nineteenth century in the Arab Gulf and Arabian Peninsula in his leadership, manners, knowledge, dealing with foreign powers, and in his ability to predict future events. Unlike almost all tribal leaders or Ottoman administrators, Sheikh Jassim never confiscated anything from defeated soldiers. In fact, he treated the soldiers of the defeated army in the Al-Wejba battle very nicely as if they were his guests. Yet their leader fled to Bahrain for his own safety.

What makes writing about such charisma so difficult is the huge bulk of writings about him, whether by his contemporaries or after his death. They all agree on the same description of his personality and his role in the politics of his time. Even if we are selective, there will be great repetitions. I was enthused in writing about Sheikh Jassim by his integrity whether in practicing pure Islamic religion or accomplishing his goal of independent Qatar. Many people, especially political leaders, practice religion by praying, fasting, etc., yet they allow themselves to violate their religious principles and ideologies by stealing, lying, or even killing innocent people. They follow a false idea: to reach your goal, one can use any means available. Since the man died long time ago, I expect no reward except from God as I present this personality to the new generation to be their role model.

A Comprehensive View of Sheikh Jassim

We would like to present a comprehensive view of Sheikh Jassim, showing his personal features and their merits. We shall also provide the status quo of the region and society in and around Qatar during the nineteenth and early twentieth centuries. The reader who is not familiar of that period of the Middle East will benefit from the book and understand why Sheikh Jassim was the star of that era. Most of what has been written about him is based on the opinions of his contemporaries, whether those who liked him or those who did not. It should be noted that Sheikh Jassim accomplished his goals in spite of the great impediments that stood against him. The following are some of these obstacles:

- There were not enough financial resources or good reasons to manifest leadership in Qatar to extend its influence to other Arab Gulf areas.
- The population of Qatar was very small, comprised of nomadic tribes that had relations with tribes of neighboring regions.
- There were no economic resources on which a solid infrastructure could be built on. Hence, government expenditure was so meager that it could not create growth in gross national product or interchange between economic sectors.
- Human resources of Qatar did not have skills that had developed through historical heritage. The society did not have clear social stratification. That is, there was no middle class that had the investors' mind. Qatar education was limited to religious classes and elementary schools.
- Qatar did not have big cities, ports, or even villages to warrant administrative authorities for law enforcement. Each sheikh of tribe handled disputes within his tribe.
- Qatar has unbearable climate and desert-type land. Lack of rain and poor soil made it extremely difficult to grow edible vegetation. The very hot and humid weather hampered any effort to work in anything.

How could it be expected of a man to lead a few tribes that were fighting with each other and maintain tribal relations with tribes outside the boundaries of Qatar? Besides, the geographical, economic, climate, and the social fabric were all the worst that one can imagine. It takes a miracle to survive in such severe conditions. However, Sheikh Jassim was able to unite those tribes under his leadership, let these tribes give him unlimited authority to speak for them, and accomplish pure independence. After his reliance on Allah's support and guidance, he used his intelligence, forbearance, honesty, and courage. His preference of the hereafter over this life led him to spend all his great wealth for good causes, including, but not limited to, administrative expenditures.

Moreover, Sheikh Jassim, who was a leader of a tiny entity, had to walk through the crossroads of great empires struggling with each other to control the Arab Gulf and the territories on its shores.

I was attracted by the character, manners, knighthood, religion adherence, integrity, and accomplishments through reading some research papers and books. I thought that there might be some room for me to dig into Ottoman documents in Istanbul to come up with a new look at this personality. Although I have several documents that were not translated from Turkish, but I think they will be added in the next addition.

Development of Leadership in Sheikh Jassim through his Belief in Monotheism

It was reported that Imam Ali bin abi Talib wrote to his governor of Basra, Abdullah bin Abbas, saying, "It was brought to my attention that you treated Beni Tamim harshly." If a star of Bani Tamim died, another star emerges. They never fell into trifles before or after Islam.

After the transgression of the Persians on Basra in 1776 and their killing of its people as well as confiscating their properties, which was labeled as Devastation of Basra, many families and tribesmen fled to Al-Ahsa'a then to Qatar. Other tribes migrated from Nejd and other parts of the Arabian Peninsula to Qatar when they had a long drought. When people were hit with human or natural atrocities, they tended to go where they had relatives or if they were welcomed by the recipient tribes.

Besides, during the period 1770–1820, there were several destructive campaigns that took place in the Arabian Peninsula led by the sons of Mohammed Ali Pasha of Egypt. These campaigns resulted in the great destruction of many cities. Tribesmen fled to the eastern regions and Qatar, especially Bani Tamim and its branches. Since these migrants came from different areas and for different reasons, they were seeking a peaceful life. They all found in Sheikh Mohammed bin Thani, Jassim's father, the leader that could bring them together. Sheikh Mohammed also had an alliance with Imam Faisal bin Turki, a very influential man among the tribes of the Arabian Peninsula. The Imam was dealing with Mohammed bin Thani as the most important chief of tribe in Qatar.

Sheikh Jassim followed his father's steps and went beyond. He began to propagate the idea of peaceful coexistence among the tribes of Qatar and the other areas of the eastern region of the Arabian Peninsula. He used his ability as a good speaker to strengthen his ties with each tribe individually. Hence, all tribal leaders in Qatar gave Sheikh Jassim their vote of confidence, forming an alliance. Sheikh Jassim left behind him people who considered themselves as citizens of Qatar rather than tribe loyalists. It gave the country an uncompromising population.

THE CALL FOR MONOTHEISM

Undoubtedly, the monotheism belief and adherence to the original Islam had their great effect on unifying the tribes of Arabian Peninsula and the western coast of the Gulf. The sheikhs of these tribes and the young generation found in pure Islamic beliefs good common ground for coming together. They also stood as a blocking stone against the anti-Islamic movements of secularism and European missionaries. The negligent Ottoman Sultan, the corrupt governors and their subordinates, and the ignorant tribal sheikhs allowed deviation from the original Islam and the spread of fables among Muslims.

The anti-Islamic groups during the eighteenth and nineteenth centuries tried to ruin the social, intellectual, and economic fabric and hampered any development process. They fabricated thousands of Prophet Mohammed sayings to sway people from the original Islam. These groups were supported financially and with other means by the Qaramita and the Boehi dynasties. These deviations from the original Islam reached its peak during the occupation of the Safavids of Iraq. They became Muslims to destroy Islam from within.

Qatar and the other areas of the Arabian Peninsula were safe from these innovations and inventions into Islam, which also resulted in creating antagonism between tribes and even families, leading to continuous fighting instead of being united under the banner of Islam as they used to be. One of the great journalists of that time, the director of *Al-Riyadh* newspaper, wrote just before the death of Sheikh Jassim:

> The people of Qatar today are the most adherent of the original Islam and its virtues among all Arab countries. They were not affected by the innovations, fables and immoral manners. The society of Qatar holds strongly to the Holy Book and the tradition of the Prophet (PBUH). Mosques had their endowments from Sheikh Jassim to take care of their expenses. Sheikh Jassim usually delivers Friday sermons and hold classes after the prayers. He has encouraged people to learn their religion, enjoined goodness and forbid atrocity. He was a great model for his people in piety, generosity, best manners and humbleness. His endowments for mosques and learning institutes were in Nejd, Al-Ahsa'a, Qassim, Bahrain, Basra and many other cities. When Sheikh Jassim gave speech or sermon, his audience would be fully attentive. When he gave money, he was very generous. When he ordered people, they obeyed his orders unquestionably.

Parturition of Leadership and God's Mercy

The Ottoman troops moved toward the eastern areas of the Arabian Peninsula and the Arab Gulf to make sure that the British would not consolidate their existence in Bahrain Oman's shores. The troops, which were led by the reformer Midhat Pasha, appointed the governor of Baghdad and Basra. Sheikh Jassim, who knew that Midhat Pasha's campaign was undoubtedly coming to Qatar and that the campaign was not against him, invited the troops to come to Qatar. His invitation was meant to avoid having the troops enter

Qatar as occupiers but as invited guests. If Midhat Pasha entered Qatar by war, he might appoint a Turkish administrator or a submissive local person. Besides, the Ottoman Sultan appreciated Sheikh Jassim's invitation in seeking the Muslims' protection from a foreign power.

Sheikh Jassim used this opportunity to connect Qatar to the Ottoman Empire while remaining the ruler of his country. He also avoided a war with a stronger army to suffer from losing casualties in a losing war like what happened in Al-Ahsa'a. Besides, if Sheikh Jassim did not invite Midhat Pasha and his army, there was a possibility that the British would make a move to occupy Qatar under the umbrella of protecting Qatar from the occupation of the Ottomans.

Views of Sheikh Jassim's Reign

The Invariable Fundamentals in Politics

Undoubtedly, Sheikh Jassim's strong adherence to the original Islam had its effects on shaping his character. Hence, his call for monotheism and his great ability to convince his audience in his speeches and sermons convinced tribal leaders to realize that unity was better for them than staying sheikhs of weak tribes. His excellent manners and knighthood distinguished him from all other sheikhs of tribes in the area. He was able, therefore, to form a solid barrier against foreign invaders, some corrupt Ottoman governors and their subordinate administrators, and some ignorant chiefs of Arabian tribes. He also prevented fables and innovations in Islam, which were widely spread in Iran, Iraq, and Syria.

By the grace of Allah, the One guided the sheikhs of tribes in the eastern region of the Arabian Peninsula and Qatar to rally behind the alliance of Sheikh Mohammed (Sheikh Jassim's father) with Sheikh Faisal bin Turki. The latter exempted Qatar from *zakat* (alms) and all other taxes.

Hence, God saved these tribes from those afflictions and guided them toward unity under the banner of Islam instead of being scattered entities, which would be liable for foreign domination. The tribes of Qatar were a good example for other tribes of the region when they formed tribal confederacy under the leadership of Sheikh Jassim. The strength or weakness of any group of tribes depends on their alliance versus disintegration.

Ibn Khaldoun[2] wrote in his *Muqadima* (introduction) about the importance of loyalty to your blood relation, tribe, or alliance of tribes, assuming that there is an interrelationship between these loyalties. Such an interrelationship leads to the feeling of each individual with the other members. Each member protects and defends his fellow members of the group as he defends himself. The individual is melted into the group to the extent of sacrificing himself for the group unselfishly. There is no difference between transgressions on any individual of the group. In other words, the *I* becomes equal to the *we*. However, this collective feeling cannot be used by an individual in aggression to others because he would be using the group for his own interest. This falls into selfishness.

It has been reported authentically that Prophet Mohammed (PBUH) told his companions, "Help your brother [fellow Muslim] if he is transgressed on or if he is transgressor." The companions asked, "We help him if he is transgressed on, but how do we help him if he is the transgressor?" The Prophet replied, "By preventing him from transgression."

To summarize Ibn Khaldoun's thought, leadership is based on a team spirit of ideology or nationalism. It has a political function of reaching the leadership and preserving it. It is like the political parties of today. The loyalty to the group by everybody leads to the betterment of the group and keeps the tribes intact. It also preserves the tribal social structure strongly through conglomeration and melting into one pot, especially against the threat of foreign power. However, if there is any internal dispute such as a transgression of one member against the other, it will be settled by the chief and the elderly men of the tribe. Ibn Khaldoun mentioned this in his *Muquadima*:

> If we examine the attitude of those who are prejudiced for their tribes, we notice that they compete with other members in giving generously,

forgive others for minor slips, forbearance during calamities, help their fellow members, honoring their promises, hospitable, religiously adherents, respecting the elderly, standing for the weak person to get his rights, etc. Any persons who is known of possessing these qualities and manners the most becomes the leader.

He added that a leader must keep track of his lineage ancestry and how he treats his own family; he puts the interests of the group before his own and reaches the top in bravery and excellent manners.

Sheikh Jassim came as an application of Ibn Khaldoun's description of an eligible leader of his tribe as well as for the alliance of tribes in Qatar. He left for the generations to follow him, an ideal pattern of how useful is the unity, a strong social fabric, collective consciousness, and the loyalty to the country. He, unfortunately, came in a tiny political entity. Hence, the renowned world historians were not aware of him and his country. If he had come in a large, well-known country, his accomplishments would have put him among the outstanding figures of history, such as Gandhi, Lenin, and Mao.

Sheikh Jassim as Viewed by

His Contemporaries

Sheikh Jassim was in the center of events that took place in the Arab Gulf and the Arabian Peninsula. There are huge numbers of documents in the Ottoman archives in Istanbul that are related to Sheikh Jassim. They included his letters to the Sultan, governors, lower-level administrators, and others. This clearly indicates his role in politics with respect to Qatar and the surrounding region.

In addition to those officials, Sheikh Jassim was popular among poets, newsmen, jurisprudents, and scientists in the Gulf, Iraq, Syria, and the Arabian Peninsula. He was the subject of some British historians and officials in Bahrain and Bushier, Iran. Since the world's means of communication were not as of today, all writings and speeches remained mostly local.

He was described by his contemporaries as a man of good characters, commendable conduct, and attractive personality. He was respectable, brave, generous, and rushed to relieve the oppressed. He supported the spread of sciences and spent a lot of money for that cause in Qatar and other areas. Just to cite few prominent persons who wrote about Sheikh Jassim as follows:

- Mohammed Shukri Al-Aloussi, a notable Iraqi historian, said, "Sheikh Jassim was among the best Arab leaders. He adheres to the Islamic religion, preserving his prayers and other obligations on time, is very knowledgeable of Islam, and has many endowments for mosques and schools. He was obeyed by his constituents."
- Mohammed Behjat Al-Athari, a great Iraqi historian and a student of Al-Aloussi, said about Sheikh Jassim that he was the greatest supporter of Islamic reform. He was among the leading persons who purified Islam from fables and undesirable innovations.

The testimony of these two renowned historians could be sufficient. But there are many other well-known personalities; we shall mention some:

- John Philbi: "Sheikh Jassim known to have a legendary reputation. He held on his bodily and mental power until his death. People used to see him in the afternoons riding a horse in the company of children and grandchildren."
- Francis Bevel Bride, the British political envoy to Bahrain, described his meeting with Sheikh Jassim in the latter's farm in 1905 by saying, "I was surprised to see a beautiful garden well organized with its pomegranate trees and about 300 palm trees. In his chamber sitting a respected Sheikh just like what you read about in the old religious books. He had a beard with some white hair. His face was

full of young vitality. Hence, he looked much younger than his actual age. He had one of his six years old children in his lap. Even though he was very strong dominating personality, he was lovable with good natured features. I noticed that he showed hospitality to his guests. He was very knowledgeable about world politics. But he kept repeating that he was retiring, so these affairs do not concern him."

- Nafith Pasha, chief administrator of Najd and former governor of Basra, had very good relation with Sheikh Jassim and used to visit Qatar often. In one of his visits, he sent a telegram to the Ottoman sultan mentioned in it, "Sheikh Jassim Al-Thani, the Administrator of Qatar District is running the District without a salary. He showed firmness and patience against British transgression. He proved his loyalty toward our Empire and assisted us during these days. Therefore, I recommend treating him graciously and with respect. We request that he will be honored with an appropriate medal of merit." The response was very quick from Istanbul as the Sultan issued the necessary proclamation in February 16, 1888.

- Suleiman bin Salih Al-Dakheel Al-Nejdi[3] was a contemporary of Sheikh Jassim. He visited Qatar in 1909 and wrote later, "Qatar is still a residence for the Arabs. It is progressing under the leadership of Sheikh Jassim Al-Thani. Its entire people are following the original Islam and their religious practice is correct. They do not have any of those innovations or additions to the original Islam. That is why you find them with good manners, piety and generosity. There commerce is growing, especially of pearls. There are about 2,500 ships of different sizes. Each village or town had a mosque. Sheikh Jassim was granted by Allah great wealth, knowledge in religion, and pious children. Even though he was in his nineties, he was energetic and can hardly be overcome in horse racing. When he gives a speech or sermon, he captures his audience. He owns 25 ships used for pearl diving. He also buys pearls from other ship owners. His total wealth is estimated at one million liras. Qatar at that time had population of about 40,000; most of them live on the pearl activities. Sheikh Jassim died July 17, 1913."

- Sheikh Abdullah Al-Bassam:[1] "Sheikh Jassim was a man of faithfulness and honor friendship for those in desperate need. He interceded with King Abdul Aziz bin Saud to free our family in 1322 Hijri (1904). Qatar, during his rule became independent, business was flourished, it erected a port, its population grew substantially and people became prosperous, especially in pearl activities. Consequently, construction sector boomed in Doha the Capital and other newly emerged cities."

- There are many other renowned personalities such as Nassir bin Jouher, Khairiddin Al-Zerkely Al-Demeshqi, the great historian and novelist Ameen Al-Rihani, and Abdul Bade'e Saqar; all of them wrote about Sheikh Jassim, praising him just like the aforementioned historians and writers.

Besides, there were many poets who wrote beautiful elegies describing Sheikh Jassim the person, the leader and the religious adherent. Among those was the poet Sheikh Hussein bin Ali Al-Nafisa and Mohammed bin Uthaimeen. Both of them give good description of his character, accomplishments, role in politics, and religious life. They indicated that his death was not only a loss for Qatar but to the Islamic world.

When the tribes of Qatar became weak and exhausted because of their wars against each other, no chief of any tribe was able to dominate over the others. After that came Sheikh Jassim, who did not fight against any other tribe. Following his father's footsteps, he began to talk to the other sheikhs of unity instead of antagonism. He used the Islamic teaching of brotherhood to advocate unity. The

---

[1] ʿHe was a religious Sheikh rather than a chief of tribe.

chiefs of tribes found in him the best leader of their allegiance. They made him their amir and spokesman. He accepted the responsibility and proved to be the man for it.

After he gained the leadership of the tribes of Qatar, he thought that he needed protection from a bigger power. There were the British, the Dutch, and the Portuguese on one hand and the Ottoman Empire on the other. He decided to resort to the latter because they were Muslims. So he requested from the Ottoman chief administrator of Nejd to come to Qatar for protection against the British station in Bahrain. However, events did not go as planned, which resulted in the killing of about two hundred soldiers. The sultan understood what happened and decided to affix Sheikh Jassim as the amir of Qatar.

Glimpses and Lessons from

Sheikh Jassim's Legacy

His name is Jassim or Qassim bin Mohammed bin Thani bin Mohammed bin Rashid bin Ali bin Sultan bin Zaid bin Sa'ad bin Salem bin A'amr bin Mi'edhad . . . bin Malik bin Zaid Munat bin Tamim from the tribe of bani Tamim Al-Mudharia Al-Adnania.[2]

His life was full of events, trials, wars, and conflicts. He passed through them successfully, relying on God's protection and guidance until he reached his goal, gaining independence for his country. We shall mention two tribulations:

The first was with Sheikh Mohammed bin Khalifa of Bahrain in 1867. The latter invited Sheikh Jassim to visit Bahrain giving him the safety. Bin Khalifa breached his promise. He imprisoned Sheikh Jassim in a fortress. However, he was able to get out and returned to Qatar; the entire population of Qatar welcomed him as a hero.

---

[2] ·The reader may wonder why the author mentioned all these ancestry. It is one of the most important pride of the Arab is their lineage of ancestry, especially if it goes to Prophet Ismail.

Consequently, Sheikh Jassim came out of this incident more beloved by his people, and the unity of tribes became stronger.

It is interesting to note that the British claimed that Bahrain violated the rules of the sea. Therefore, they invaded Bahrain, burning all its ships and bombarding the fortress where bin Khalifa used to live in. He escaped to save himself. But his brother Ali and his sons overthrew Mohammed bin Khalifa and imprisoned him in the same fortress he held Sheikh Jassim in. Hence, what was planned by bin Khalifa against Sheikh Jassim turned into the destruction of the Khalifa family, which was ruling Bahrain.

The second tribulation was the Al-Wejba battle. This event will be elaborated on in chapter 7. The Ottoman governor of Basra, Hafidh Pasha, led a campaign to destroy the political structure of Qatar and get rid of Sheikh Jassim. The war ended with a victory of Qatar and its leader, Sheikh Jassim. While Hafidh Pasha fled to a British ship, Qatar was granted independence under the leadership of Sheikh Jassim.

Among Sheikh Jassim's commendable stances was his telegram to the sultan requesting him to cancel the military campaign against bin Saud, who had a dispute with bin Rasheed. He asked the sultan to refrain from deepening the dispute. Sheikh Jassim mentioned in the telegram that the sultan should listen to his subordinates, who were known for their efficiency and integrity. Hence, Sheikh Jassim used his standing with the sultan to prevent unnecessary war, like what happened in the Dar'ieh in which the sultan relied on reports from the sharif of Mecca and the governor of Baghdad.

To cite one of the incidents of generous hospitality of Sheikh Jassim toward that nobility who were inflicted with a calamity was his welcoming Abdul Rahman Al-Faisal and his family. Sheikh Jassim sent a message to Abdul Rahman's son, saying, "When your father and his family arrived, I ordered the women of Al-Thani to leave their rooms, furniture, clothes and jewelry for the guests. Every day they were my guests, it was a celebration day."

According to Lorimar and Al-Zerkely, the imam Abdul Rahman Al-Faisal stayed in Qatar for more than three months, June–August 1892.

Sheikh Jassim possessed the characteristics and dignity of leadership as they appear in a great leader. When the British commander Colonel Ross visited Sheikh Jassim 1888, he received his guest with seven hundred horse riders. It was a fantastic show that indicated the alliance of Qatar population behind their leader, giving him the legal authority of Qatar.

Ross described Sheikh Jassim to be different than other sheikhs of the Arab Gulf: "It was customary that sheikhs visit British Commander on the deck of a ship. But I was certain that Sheikh Jassim whose personality was full of suspicion would refuse. Hence, he would not come to a ship."

Dr. G. F. Paterson, the historian and political analyst specializing in the Arab Gulf and the Arabian Peninsula, wrote the following:

> The British colonization of India made it interested in the Gulf during the 19th century and the first half of the 20th century. The British authorities tried to establish maritime treaties between the coastal political entities. . . . The course of history in western shores of the Gulf and eastern area of the Arabian Peninsula were not determined by the British, but by local notable personalities such as Sheikh Jassim bin Mohammed Al-Thani.

Sheikh Jassim was afflicted in his wealth when the British, especially their resident in Bushier, Iran, exaggerated in pressing on Qatar and its leader, Sheikh Jassim. They cost Qatar a great deal in curtailing its pearl trading. The British finally used the incident of Sheikh Jassim's expulsion of the Indian merchants, the Banyan, because they were considered British subjects. They confiscated Sheikh Jassim's movable assets and withheld his ships in Bahrain and Bombay.

His other affliction was the assassination of his son, Ali. He was the most beloved son for he was pious and brave. He was killed in 1886 during a transgression of a tribe at night on Doha when people were sleeping. Sheikh Jassim was in Al-Dha'ayn where he resided.

Sheikh Jassim used pearl activity as his business. It was very profitable business in those days. He had thirty ships, which he used for pearl divers. Besides, he was financing other shipowners and used to buy pearls for trading. His business let him accumulate great wealth, which he used to finance his government, help the needy, and purchase property for mosques and schools. With his generosity and him being the leading sheikh in Qatar, his family used to spend a great deal as there were guests all year round.

Sheikh Jassim used to give a sermon and lead the prayer on Friday. He had the habit of holding a class after the prayer on religious subjects. He also used to invite Islamic scholars to be guest speakers in Qatar.

Excerpts from Sheikh Jassim's Will

In the name of Allah the most Beneficent most Merciful.

All praise is to Allah, the Lord of the worlds (mankind, jinn and all that exist), and no assault except on the oppressors. May peace and blessings be on the most honorable among the messengers our master Mohammed, peace be upon him, his relatives and his companions.

From Qassim bin Mohammed to his honorable brother Jebr bin Mohammed and my sons Khalifa, Thani, Abdullah, Abdul Rahman and Mohammed may Allah save you from whims and make you pious. May peace be on you and may Allah grant you his Mercy and Blessings.

I am Qassim wrote my will during my life as I am fully intact and sound. But I do not know when I will die. I bear witness that there is no deity worthy of worship except Allah Who had no partner and I bear witness that Mohammed is his servant and Messenger. Jesus is from Allah's Breath and His word was casted on Marry. Jesus is Allah servant and messenger. Ibrahim is Allah's intimate friend, His servant and messenger. Allah spoke to Moses. Moses is Allah's servant and messenger. I believe in Allah, His angels, His holey books, His messengers and in the determination being in the Hands of Allah, whether good or bad. I bear witness that Allah is true, His threat is true, paradise is true, hellfire is true, death is true, the Hour is undoubtedly coming and Allah will resurrect all those in the graves. I have passed the median age. Prophet Mohammed, peace is upon him, said, "My Muslim nation have ages between 60 and 70, but few of them who will pass that range." I ask Allah for the best destiny.

My advice to you is; first and for most is to turn to Allah's religion in secrecy and public and to hold on firmly to the Holy Book and the tradition of His Messenger (PBUH). Allah to who is ascribed all Perfection and Majesty mentioned in the Quran, "O you who believe fear Allah as He should be feared and die not except in the state of Islam."[4] And He must be obeyed and mentioned all the time and be thanked. Allah also said, "O you who believe! Fear Allah and keep your duty to Him. And let every person look to what he was sent forth for the morrow, and fear Allah. Verily Allah is All-Aware of what you do."[5]

It is the Day when no wealth or off springs will benefit the person, but his meeting Allah with clean heart, that is good deeds. Allah mentions, "O mankind! Be afraid of your Lord and fear a day when no father can avail aught for his son, or a son avail aught for his father. Verily, the Promise of Allah is true, let not then this present life deceives you, or let the chief deceiver (Satan) deceives you about Allah."[6]

Allah enjoins on His servants; knowledge of about Him, His religion, His prophets and grasp on the testimony of "No deity worthy of worship except Allah." You should work hard to learn what this testimony means so you deny any association of partner with Allah and to devote your worship to Him and Him alone. Allah does not accept from His creations except the pure devotion for Him as Prophet Mohammed (PBUH) said about Allah, "I am not in need of being associated with others in anything. If someone associates a partner with Me, I will let him with his partner."[7] Allah mentions in the Quran, "Verily! Allah forgives not setting partner in worship with Him, but He forgives whom He pleases sins other than that, and whoever sets up partners in worship with Allah, had indeed strayed far away."[8] And He said, "Anyone associates partner with Allah, He will deprive him from Paradise and will abide in the Hellfire." Allah must be worshiped as He prescribed and not the way anyone likes to worship; adding innovations to the religion.

I look forward Allah's rewards, to abstain from His disobedience and avoid His punishment. Be aware that Allah has guaranteed your sustenance. He mentions in the Quran, "And in heaven is your provision, and that which you are promised."[9] From this you should realize not to prefer any action of this life over that of the Hereafter.

Allah mentions, "O' you who believe! Let not your properties or your children divert you from the remembrance of Allah. And whosoever does that, and then they are the losers."[10]

Any person curses Sheikh Mohammed bin Abdul Wahhab, his followers or his beliefs as if he degraded me and betrayed me.

SHEIKH JASSIM'S POETRY

Sheikh Jassim was an excellent poet. There is in the Arabic text a poem by Sheikh Jassim, which he composed during the Al-Wejba battle, when the governor of Basra and some hirelings Arabs attacked Qatar in the fasting month of Ramadan 1310 Hijri (1892). Most of the poem was turning to Allah for assistance and to give him and his troops the strength against the transgressors. In the Arab tribal wars, it is normal to chant poetry, especially in colloquial language, during the battle to enhance the fighters' strength and patience. It became more effective when it came from the leader himself. There are many other poems for Sheikh Jassim in the book, which I (the translator) find it unnecessary to translate. The poem loses its strength with the translation.

* * *

CHAPTER 2

PREAMBLE AND HISTORICAL BACKGROUND

Geographical Setting

Qatar has been, through history, the focus of keen invaders and those who were concerned about the security of the Arab Gulf. It has been one of the keys to control the Arab Gulf. Hence, its location has an importance in geopolitics.

In a report submitted to the Ottoman sultan Abdul Majeed in 1850 stressed the significance of Qatar because it is situated between Nejd and Bahrain, Ha'el, and Oman. It is the open window to the Gulf of Basra, the anterior region of the Arabian Peninsula and the Indian Ocean.

Qatar is a peninsula that extends into the Arab Gulf[11] as a long tongue followed by several Islands. Qatar is connected with the eastern coast of the Arabian Peninsula only from the southern part of the country.

The land of Qatar is flat with a rocky surface. There are some limy hills in the west and Mount Foyirit in the north. They are in the northern and central regions many swamps, ponds, and pans, which accumulate water from the rain. The areas around them are fertile.

Total area of Qatar is 11,521 square kilometers. It was formed mostly through the drying of shallow water of the Gulf, which merged into the mainland. Al-A'deed and Al-Khor are example of these newly formed lands. There are many sand dunes along the coast. The internal region of Qatar Peninsula is a low plain with some small hills. The highest point of these hills is 103 meters above sea level, while the lowest point of that region is about 6 meters below sea level.

The land is very dry with little rain, which comes only in the winter. The surface is exposed to the high temperature of the sun. This turns the surface into a lime layer. It makes it very difficult to plant anything, except in the north where there is green vegetation. The latter area contains grass, pasture, and scattered trees and palm trees. The southern region is covered with sand.

Qatar has a long summer, with temperature passing 120°F in the shade for most of the summer. Temperature starts to get down in September. Winter is warm with little rain. They are the best months of the year. The country is affected by the northwest and southeast winds. The weather becomes nice during the time when the northwest wind blows. The weather becomes hot and humid with the southeast wind. Sandstorms often come during the summer, making life miserable.

HISTORICAL SETTING OF THE ARAB GULF REGION

The Arabs had occupied both the western and eastern shores of the Arab Gulf and all the islands in it since thousands of years before Christ. Recorded history never referred to other nations or people to be in or either shore of the Gulf. The Arabs established their political entities, built their culture and tradition. They had, for example, their regalities such as the Kingdom of Kerkh Missan in Al-Ahwaz at the left side of the Shatt-el-Arab River extending to the eastern shore of the Gulf and the Kingdom of Arabian Hermes in the southern region of the Gulf, which also controlled all islands in the Gulf and the Arabian Sea. Besides, the Kan'anians, who were Semite Arabs, were the first to reside on the shores of the Gulf.

Some tribes migrated from Yemen after the collapse of the Ma'arab Dam in 120 BC to the Arab Gulf. Besides, there were several waves of migration by Arabian tribes from the Arabian Peninsula to the Gulf because of droughts. They occupied both shores of the Gulf, claiming their territorial independence.

British and Dutch documents indicate that the Kingdom of Arabian Hermes extended its control beyond their territory of the southern region of the Gulf to all the islands and both shores of the Arab Gulf. Besides, many Arab tribes lived in the eastern shores of the Gulf and the internal area for thousands of years. They established their tribal entities and emirates south of the Persian Plateau, which the Iranians used to consider their southern boundaries. During the reign of Ridha Shah and his son Mohammed (the last shah of Iran), they used the most severe ethnic cleansing with the Arabs by forcing them to migrate to the north of Iran and replacing them with Iranians.

The German historian Kerstin Nibour, who visited the Gulf in 1762, proved the aforementioned fact. In his book *Journeys in the Arabian Peninsula and Other Countries in the East*, published in 1772, he wrote, "I cannot pass by in silence without talking about the Arabian region that has importance. Though the area is located outside the desert Arabian Peninsula, the people are closer to being Arabs than any other; I mean that those who reside in the south-eastern shore of the Gulf, they belong to the same Arab of the Arabian Peninsula. But it is a laughing matter that European geographers described the residents of that area being under the submission of the Persians. There are Arabian tribes resided in the eastern coastal plain of the Gulf and the numerous island of the Gulf. These Arabs were there long before the Islamic conquest. They had their independent political emirates."

Kerstin believed that these political entities were established at the same time of the early era of the kings of Persia. "Their language was Arabic; their habits and ancestry were Arabic too. We found them craving for freedom just like the Arab Bedouins. They defended their political entity in death defiance without seeking help from others."

He also said that "this coast has never been under the rule of Persian kings. The Persians did not prefer to live in the barren coast over the Iranian Plateau. Nadir Shah, one of the Persian kings, drew a plan during his last few days of rule to force the Arabs who lived in the eastern coast of the Gulf to move to the coast of the Qazvin Sea, while replacing them by Persians. But, he was killed before he accomplished his plan." Later on, that plan was carried out by the last two shahs. It should be noted that the Persians were not a maritime nation.

The Sumerian historical documents about the era 3000 BC indicate that they reached Mejan (currently Oman) to bring copper from the southeastern region of the Arabian Peninsula. From the historical documents of the Sumerians, Babylonians, and Assyrians, one can find mention of the Kingdom of Dilmon in Bahrain. It was described as being like a fish in the middle of the sea. Dilmon was a commercial center between Mesopotamia and beyond on one hand and Mejan and the Sind Valley of India on the other. These documents show stamps indicating from where the commodities came.

From the archeological remnants, there were evidences of settlements that go back seven thousand years on the coast of Oman. In these settlements, they found pieces of black pottery, which were brought from Mesopotamia. Hence, there were quite sizable commercial activities between Mesopotamia through the Gulf to the Arabian Sea and the Indian Ocean. Although agricultural products were in abundance in Mesopotamia, people were in need for other products, such as wood, minerals, and stones. Hence they used their boats or ships through the rivers then the Gulf to take exchange their commodities with what they needed.

The Mijani (Omani) sailors dominated the trade between Mesopotamia and India during the third-century BC. People of Dilmon and other coastal cities were taking their trades through the Gulf and Mesopotamia to the Mediterranean. Their trade consisted of herbs, spices, gum, cloth materials, jewelry, precious stones, ceramic, teak, cedar, copper, and last but not least, pearls, which the Gulf was famous for.

Centuries later witnessed wars between political entities of the Mediterranean and those of southwest Asia. But the Arabs stayed away from those wars. Hence, their trade by caravans and ships continued to both regions.

Following the emergence of Islam in the seventh century, the situation in the Arab Gulf and the adjacent regions changed drastically. The Islamic nation was in full control of commercial routes across the Arab Gulf, the Red Sea, and later on, the Mediterranean as well as land routes in Iraq, Syria, Egypt, and Turkey. In the mid eighth century, the Islamic nation extended from West Africa and Spain in the west to the Sind River in India eastward.

The Arab merchants dominated trade within the east and between the east and the west until the fifteenth century, when Fiasco de Gama sailed around South Africa. He opened a new route for Europeans to reach India. Then the Arabs entered into competition with European ship captains. The Arabs were way ahead of the European geographers and explorers in the knowledge of world geography. Some of the Arab geographers and explorers were given free rides by merchants.

Mohammed bin Houqal, an explorer from Baghdad, in the tenth century, wrote his book *The Picture of the Earth*, describing the water of the Arab Gulf as very clear that one could see the white stones of its bottom. He also mentioned the existence of pearls and corals.

The geographer Al-Maqdissi described the sailors with whom he traveled as being very knowledgeable about the sea and its ports. They knew about the wind and the islands.

It has been proven that the Arab merchants used to have regular voyages to China. The Chinese also had their commercial fleet that made its trips to the Arab Gulf and East Africa.

At the beginning of the sixteenth century, the Portuguese were able to reach India through the Cape of Good Hope. They quickly set foot on their empire in the East. In 1507, a Portuguese fleet led by

Captain Kirk took over Mascot, Sahar, Khor Fakkan, and Hermes. The governor of Hermes signed a treaty of loyalty to the Portuguese Majesty. In 1521, Bahrain was seized by the Portuguese also. The Arabs suffered a great deal when the Portuguese maintained control over most of the Arab Gulf.

The invaders treated the residents very harshly with hostility and a grudge. After this agony and humiliation that the Arabs had suffered from the Portuguese, the Ottoman Empire emerged as an Islamic power that took upon itself the liberation of Islamic entities and its protection against foreign invaders. The Ottomans started by expulsion of the Persian Safavids who were occupying Iraq. The Ottoman sultan Suleiman Al-Qanouni took over Baghdad in 1534. His troops went after that to liberate Basra. The troops then went further southward to engage in a war with the Portuguese from 1538 to 1557, until they expelled them from the entire areas of the Arab Gulf, the Arabian Sea, and the Red Sea.

To summarize, the Arabs were residing and ruling both shores of the Arab Gulf and the plains beyond them—from Basra to Oman, including Arabstan, which is now occupied by the Persians. I refer the reader to the map at the end of the book.

Before we end this section, we should mention that the Gulf has had several names throughout history. The Assyrians, Babylonians, and the Acadians called it the Bitter Sea or the Southern Sea. The Chaldeans, who controlled Mesopotamia in the seventh century BC, called it the Chaldean Sea. It was also named the Persian Sea. It was mentioned that when the representative of Alexander the Great, Amir of the Sea Niarcus returned from India along the eastern coast of the Gulf. Alexander the Great called it the Persian Gulf. He apparently did not know that the Arabs were residing there, while the Persians were way up north. However, the name was circulated to the west by the Greeks.

The Gulf was called Basra Gulf because it ended at Basra. It was also called Qatif Sea. The latter is a city in the eastern region of the

Arabian Peninsula near the Gulf.[3] The reader may see the maps at the end of the book.

HISTORICAL DEVELOPMENT OF QATAR

After the Islamic nation took over Al-Yamama, which Qatar was part of, in the year 633; the entire district was part of the Islamic nation for several centuries. However, there were several mutinous rebellions during the Omayyad and Abbasside dynasties. But the most significant secessions from the Abbasside Dynasty were the Akhdharyeen, who established their state in Al-Yamama, including Qatar. The other secession was by the Qaramides. They established their state in the area between Basra in the north and Qatar and Bahrain in the south, until they were defeated in 1075. After that, tribes were weak and lived marginally.

After several centuries, the Jibour tribe, which has been one of the largest tribes in the Middle East, began to gain strength. It took over Al-Ahsa'a and Qatif in about 1470. The Jibour continued to expand until it was defeated by the Portuguese, who killed their leader Ajwad bin Zamil in Bahrain.

Another event took place in the region was that Beni Mughamis, who were ruling Basra, returned to Bahrain to rule it, expelling who were left of the Jibour. Their sheikh, Rashid bin Mughamis, controlled Al-Ahsa'a and Qatif in 1532. Following the control of the Jibour to the region, many of its branches migrated to the region from Iraq, Syria, and other places of the Middle East. When Sheikh Rashid bin Mughamis found that he was unable to face the Portuguese, he requested help from the Ottoman sultan to fight the foreign invaders.

Later on, Beni Hameed came to assist Beni Mughamis. With time, things did not go well between Beni Hameed and the Ottomans. The former expelled the latter from Al-Ahsa'a in 1673. Beni Hameed continued to rule the region until 1776.

---

3   .

The region suffered from a period of sluggishness and economic stagnation. This situation was the same in the entire Islamic area from Spain and North Africa through Iraq, the Arabian Peninsula, and the Arab Gulf. It marked the end of the Abbasids Dynasty, the rule of the Muslim in Spain, and the invasion of the Portuguese and the British. Tribes were fighting with each other for territories. There was no security because each tribe could do whatever it wanted. Hence, trade declined, and economic condition was deteriorating. Most people left the religion of Islam entirely or were using pick-and-choose with additions and superstitions.

In the throng of this mess in the Arabian Peninsula and the Gulf, God foreordained a reformer, Sheikh Mohammed bin Abdul Wahhab Al-Timimi.[12] Before long, the Arabian Peninsula united under the banner of his call for monotheism. He had difficulty convincing everybody because the superstitions and fables were set deeply in the hearts and minds of people, but gradually he was successful.

Toward the end of the eighteenth century and the beginning of the nineteenth century, the first and second reigns of the Saudis were able to control the Arabian Peninsula. They adopted the Wahhabi doctrine.

The Migration of the Ma'adhid to Qatar

It is known historically that the Ma'adhid in Qatar were from bani Tamim, the largest tribe in the Arab world. Most of the people of Qatar are the offspring of Salem bin Amr bin Mi'dhad, except a group called A'al bu Kawara, who are from Salem's brother Mushrif.

I personally received from the honorable Sheikh Jassim bin Thani, the grandson of Sheikh Jassim, the founder of Qatar, a document about migration of the Ma'adid to Qatar in which he said, "The Emirate of the Ma'adid was from the children of Sief Al-Ma'adid. He had three children; Ali, who had a son by the name Thamir. The latter was nicknamed Thamir Al-Nehshali. Most of the people of Qatar were the off springs of Thamir. The other son was Jum'a to whom bani Muqbil belong. The third son was Salama who became the first Governor of Bahrain."

Bin Fadhil mentioned that residents of Azwa and Fariha in Qatar were the offspring of the Ma'adid. They were referred to as the children of Salim bin A'mr bin Mi'dhad. His brother Mushrif had his offspring in Nejd. He also mentioned that his ancestors went from Nejd to reside for some time between Basra City and Zubair. After that, they returned to Qatar to reside in Al-Zibara and Al-Fariha. Some of them moved to Fouyrit and Doha in the beginning of the nineteenth century.

Lorimar mentioned in his memoirs, "As to their craft, the Ma'adid were pearl divers, navigators and camels and livestock breeders. Their Sheikh of tribe was Jassim bin Thani. He was the most important personality in Qatar Peninsula."[13]

Regarding the migration of Ma'adid to Qatar, it was reported that they moved from Al-Eshaiqir in Nejd to Bereen in the south of Al-Ahsa'a. From there they went to Salwa in Qatar. Some of them moved to Sebek in the southern region of Qatar, and another group went to Roweis then Zibara. These migrations were around the year 1112 Hijri (AD 1700). It was reported that the Ma'adhid migrated to Qatar before their tribal-related Al-Thani. The latter also came from Al-Eshaiqir. There is a cavern called Bareed, who was one of Sief bin Mohammed . . . bin Mi'dhad who migrated to Qatar. The cavern is a rocky shore inside the sea, curved like a big cave.

Sheikh Jassim bin Mohammed bin Thani stated that the Ma'adhid and A'al bu Kawara migrated to Qatar before the eighteenth century. They settled in a valley named after them. Then they moved to Yebreen. They had wars with Beni A'aqil until the latter seized to exist except for remnants by 1779, which were taken care of by Beni Hameed. There were a group of people from Beni Muslims whose chief was Abdulla bin Hussein . . . bin Muslim Al-Jebri. From them was Ajwad bin Zamil in Al-Ahsa'a ,who used to collect taxes from Qatar.[3]

If we go back to the events of the eighteenth century, when Basra suffered from huge destruction in 1776, the wars between tribes and the transgression of the sons of Mohammed Ali Pasha and their destruction of many cities throughout the Arabian Peninsula, which we referred to earlier, all that and much more led the Arabs to look for a way out of this mess. Hence, the tribes in Qatar, as those elsewhere, were looking for a savior who would bring them together. That was the reason for choosing Sheikh Jassim to be their unifying leader as they found in his personality and his call for monotheism what they needed.

Economic Condition of Qatar

Yaquote Al-Hamawi, the renowned geographer, indicated the importance of Qatar in trade since old ages. It used to raise good camels to be sold in its market.

Fairouz Abadi mentioned about Qatar that it was famous in its beautiful clothes, good camels, and the production of swords.

Before the discovery of oil and natural gas, the sea was the main source of income for the people of Qatar. Its economy was mainly based on pearl diving and fishing. Of course, there were many other activities relating to these two main activities, such as shipbuilding, ship repair, trading pearls and fish, and exporting pearls. There were few people working in agriculture because of the scarcity of water and rain as well as the unsuitable land for cultivation. There were some people working in handicrafts, such as textiles, and others in animal husbandry.

Market Size and Money Exchange

The economy of Qatar before the oil and natural gas bonanza was based on primary industries: pearls diving, fishing, primitive agriculture, and handicrafts. It was underdeveloped with very limited entrepreneurial initiative. Savings from these activities were reinvested in expanding means of production within the activities they were made in. For example, in a good season of pearls, the owner of the ship used to think of buying more ships rather than establish a factory. Such economy is expected to have limited size of market. Commercial relations with India, the Arabian Peninsula, Iraq, and Iran were breathing areas to exchange pearls for other commodities needed in Qatar. Besides, economic activities, size of the market, and capital circulation depended on the following:

- Money in circulation, which facilitated commodity exchange.
- There were several different currencies in the market that were accepted by sellers and buyers within Qatar and with merchants in other countries such as India and Iran. Besides, there were money exchangers (called *Sarrafs*) with whom anybody could exchange any currency for another. For example, there were the Indian rupee, the Ottoman lira, the French rial, the Omani pazeh, etc.
- The Ottoman lira was about 20 percent of the Indian rupee. Every 5 French rials (it was called Maria Teresa Rial)[3] equaled 7 Indian rupees. These rates varied from time to time depending on the price of gold and size of trade between Qatar and each country.

Merchants also used commodity barter.

The Ottoman government realized the importance of currency and its usage. Hence, it issued an order for all governors and their subordinates to use the lira in all their transactions, whether official or not. The Ottoman government also issued a law of determining weights using the decimal system. This could have been useful if it was applied throughout the Ottoman Empire. But people continued to use weights they were accustomed to using.

People in Qatar were using certain traditions in their commercial transactions. Besides, personal relations between buyers and sellers dominated the market exchange of commodities. For example, a person may buy a sack of rice without paying for it, because the seller knew that he would pay for it when he had money. People trusted each other so much that there would not be any recording of the transactions. Sheikh Jassim was able to use that to slip away from Ottoman tax laws and custom duties, which were vicious tools in the hands of some Ottoman officials to use against whom they disliked.

In order to give an idea about the economy of Qatar during the Ottoman era, we shall discuss the activities of maritime activities concentrating on pearl diving and other activities.

MARITIME ACTIVITIES

Maritime activities included pearl diving, fishing, sea transportation, sea trade, ship building, and repairing and marketing of pearls and fish. These activities gave the majority of the population.

Pearl diving and its trade used to provide income for the largest segment of the population. It was the most profitable activity too. Although pearl activities created a group of very high income, their savings remained within the activity. Besides, they did not invest in improving the activity but duplicated what they had of facilities. Moreover, Sheikh Jassim, who controlled a high percentage of the pearl diving and trading, used to spend most of his earnings on government administrative expenses and the endless guests as being the chief of tribal alliance.

Pearl diving was the most dangerous and life-threatening activity, especially for the divers. They used to submerge to the bottom of the sea to collect oysters that contained pearls. Often a diver continued to pick oysters, especially if he found a large number of them but found out that he was unable to reach the surface.

Bairouni wrote in his book *Aljawahir fi Ma'arifet aljawahir* that the pearl divers found it very difficult to stay a long time under the surface. Hence, they invented an apparatus made of leather. They filled it with air and tied it to their abdomens. It had an opening that was tied to their noses to breathe from while underwater. This apparatus enabled the diver to stay even days under water, except for food and drink.

It is known that pearls are found in oysters that live in warm water seas. The Arab Gulf was the source of the best pearls. The process of getting pearls had a pyramided organization. The diving ship or boat had a team consisting of five to twenty-five members, depending on its size. Each member of the team had his specific job in a well-organized system. Before the ship set for sailing, the owner made sure that they had enough food, water, and other things they needed for their trip, which usually used to take four months. The following is a description of the function of members of the team:

1. The captain was the chief of the crew. He was the most knowledgeable about the sea, the area where they could find more oysters, the timing of the wind, etc. He had to be obeyed by everyone else; otherwise they all might be in danger.
2. The divers were those who used to submerge to the bottom of the sea to pick the oysters. They tied a rock to their feet to help them plunge down. They carried with them small nets to put the oysters in, which was tied by a rope with a person on deck. The diver was tied by a rope with a person on deck to pull the diver upon his signaling. Since the job of the diver was the most dangerous and he was the one who fetched the provision, he got the highest percentage of the proceeds.
3. The *seeb* was the person who pulled the diver and the oysters' net up to the deck.
4. The *radhifa* were young boys who used to do light duties. They were there to get training for future jobs. They were paid wages.
5. The cook, the chanter, and other helpers were paid wages.

The captain usually had the money to finance the trip. He purchased all that the crew needed during the trip and gave his crew members money to leave with their families when they were in the trip, because they could stay as long as four months.

At the end of the diving season, the captain would sell the pearls to a merchant. He would divide the proceeds among the members of his crew according to the known ratios and wages. The pearls might be sold to another merchant or exporter.

A pearl hunting ship.

According to an Ottoman document, pearl season was from May 1 to August 31. Sheikh Jassim used to buy pearls directly from captains or from merchants. Besides, he had the largest fleet of ships of his own. Mostly, he exported the pearls he had to Bombay, India. These documents indicated that there were about three thousand ships in Qatar, mostly small ones. They provided the people with great deal of income.

OTHER ECONOMIC ACTIVITY

Among the other activities was trade. Qatar's geographic location made it very suitable as a trade center. It is between Bahrain, Oman, Arabian Peninsula, and Iraq. Maritime trade and camel caravans passed by it. Besides, Qatar was producing textiles and swords, raising good quality of camels and horses in addition to pearls.

Qatar also had some agricultural products for its own consumption.

There is some information about the economy of Qatar that was recorded in a letter sent from the Ottoman deputy administrator of Qatar, District of the Ottoman sultan, dated November 26, 1892. He mentioned in the letter that income generated from pearl diving in Qatar reached 2,540,000 liras. Sheikh Jassim collected pearl-diving taxes, *zakat* (alms) on animals, and slaughtering duties totaled 77,403 liras.

The following table was prepared by the Ottoman administrator of Nejd—more detailed information about the economy of Qatar. It should be noted that these figures were rough estimates because he had no way of knowing the information except by asking chiefs of tribes about it. They had every reason to underestimate the figures to avoid taxes and duties.

TABLE 1
STATISTICAL DATA OF QATAR

ENTRIES	ESTIMATES
Population	20,000
Urban dwellers	8,000
Rural dwellers	12,000
Number of mosques in the cities	19
Number of mosques in rural areas	15
Number of elementary schools	15
Number of pearl diving ships (all sizes)	335
Number of workers on commercial ships	5,350
Tax per person working on large commercial ships (liras)	5.8
Tax per person working on medium and small ships (liras)	8.0
Total income generated from pearl diving (liras)	2,540,000
Number of sheep and goats	17,000
Zakat (alms) on animals (liras)	17,000

Number of camels	2,000
ENTRIES	**ESTIMATES**
Duties on animal slaughtering (Liras)	1,883
Taxes paid by merchants (Liras)	44,825
Taxes paid on sea products (Liras)	9,900
Number of animals imported from Iran	9,000
Number of animals taken as taxes in kind	900
Imported rice (sacs)	20,000
Total value of the imported rice (Liras)	1,200,000
Imported wheat (sacs)	4,000
Total value of the imported wheat (Liras)	240,000
Imported barley (sacs)	1,000
Total value of the imported barley (Liras)	50,000
Imported coffee (sacs)	500
Value of the imported coffee (Liras)	30,000
Imported sugar (sacs)	2,000
Total value of the imported sugar (Liras)	120,000

In addition to what is mentioned in table 1, Qatar imported tobacco at twenty thousand liras from Iran and Oman, oil at eight thousand liras from Kuwait, Bahrain, Iran, Qatif, burning oil at 1,500 liras, and a few other quantities of clothes, charcoal, etc.

It should be noted that there was some conflict between Sheikh Za'id of Abu Dhabi and Sheikh Jassim of Qatar regarding the taxes on pearl diving near the Omani coast. The residents of Oman felt closer in blood relation to the people of Qatar. They wanted their protection, hence were paying taxes to Sheikh Jassim. Yet Sheikh Za'id considered the diving activities were in Abu Dhabi's sea waters. Hence, the taxes should have been collected by him. Consequently, the Omanis were paying both sheikhs taxes.

CHAPTER 3

POLITICAL CONDITION PRIOR TO SHEIKH JASSIM'S EMERGENCE

SECTION 1

OTTOMANS AS THE NEW POWER

IN THE ARAB GULF

If we go back to recent history of the Arab Gulf and the Arabian Peninsula regions and examine the social and political conditions, we would have better understanding of what happened in Qatar and the emergence of its founder Sheikh Jassim. Such studies are necessary to comprehend what seem vague circumstances during the last three centuries that resulted into the formation of the current political entities.

We shall discuss the events that took place in Basra, Nejd, Al-Ahsa'a, Bahrain, and the coast of Oman. We shall refer to the notable persons who made their marks in the history of the region. It is also very important to throw light on the struggles among the tribes and the infiltration of the British into the region. All that led to give rise to charisma, which brings everybody under his umbrella.

The Arab Gulf and the Red Sea were the maritime routes of trade between the East and the West. They formed the bases for commercial and cultural exchange between India and China on one end, and the civilizations of Arab Gulf and Mesopotamia as well as Europe on the other hand. The Arab Gulf region was the crossroads of ancient civilization because it is located at the end of the Fertile Crescent, that is, the green land whose other end is the River Nile Delta.

The Expulsion of the Portuguese

There were two reasons for the Ottomans to charge with their troops and ships toward the Red Sea and the Arab Gulf: first, their power intensity and their awakening, and secondly, the provocation of the Portuguese of the way they treated Muslim commercial ships. The Portuguese controlled the Indian Ocean then moved to control the Arab Gulf. They mistreated Muslims and degraded Islam in the areas they controlled. They had no morals. For example, Ibn Majid, the great Arab explorer, showed the Portuguese Fiasco de Gamma the road through the Cape of Good Hope in the early sixteenth century. Instead of thanking him for the service, they killed him to declare that the Portuguese were the discoverers of the route around South Africa.

The Portuguese took advantage of the weakness of the Arab tribes that resided at the coasts of Indian Ocean, Arabian Sea, and the Arab Gulf, which encouraged them to continue occupying those coastal areas. However, the Portuguese were thought of as crossing the red lines when they took over Jeddah and threatened to attack Mecca and Medina. The Ottomans could not take it anymore. Besides, they were hijacking Muslims' commercial ships, confiscating their merchandise, and torturing the captain and his crew by cutting their noses then killing them. Hence, all Muslim merchants stopped going through that route. Consequently, the Ottoman sultan was aroused.

He considered that it was his duty to put an end to the Portuguese aggression.

In the year 1517, the Ottoman sultan Saleem the First took over Egypt and established the Ottoman authority over the Red Sea. With that, he reopened the commercial route from the Indian Ocean to the Mediterranean Sea.

The Ottomans undertook the responsibility of facing a strong knowledgeable enemy by fighting it in the Indian Ocean. They felt that they were strong enough for the job. If the Ottomans, who claimed being the leader of the Islamic nation, did not take the responsibility, who would?

The Portuguese were using inhumane and cruel practices of taking over territories as they frightened people to surrender. They were cutting noses and cutting limbs of Muslims before they killed them. That made residents of coastal areas hate them and collaborate with any savior.

The Ottomans were concerned about the Muslims and defended them out of sharing the same spiritual beliefs. But after 1517, the Ottomans considered themselves the inheritors of the Islamic caliphate. Therefore, their defense was their first responsibility as they were defending their own constituents. The Ottoman Empire in the sixteenth century possessed millions of square kilometers in territories in the Middle East and Europe.

Muslim merchants were buying spices, textiles, perfumes, raw materials, and manufactured goods from India, China, and other Eastern countries to sell them to European countries. They were using the route through the Indian Ocean, the Arabian Sea, the Red Sea, and finally, the Suez Gulf. After that, they used land transport to Alexandria from which they went through the Mediterranean Sea toward Istanbul then Europe. They were making very high income until the Portuguese interfered in the Muslim merchants' trade in a piracy type of practice.

For these reasons, the Ottomans embarked on serious and courageous campaigns to stop the Portuguese. They entered into a long maritime war. It should be noted that when Sultan Salim the First took over Egypt, the person who led the Ottoman war fleet was Beari Ra'ees.[14]

Captain Beari Ra'ees entered the Red Sea from the Suez as being the captain of Egypt in the year 1551. He crossed the Red Sea with the Ottoman fleet, which consisted of thirty ships going toward the Arab Gulf.

When Captain Ra'ees took over the Port of Masqat on the Omani coast, he ended the control of the Portuguese in the Red Sea and the Arabian Sea, which continued for forty years. He block-aded Hormuz Island. When he was just about to take it over, the Portuguese offered him a great deal of gifts in return for lifting the blockade from the island. He collected the great wealth and sailed off to Basra. However, he heard that that the Portuguese were planning to attack him. He put the wealth in three of his ships and sailed toward Egypt. His intention was to take the wealth to Istanbul, but his enemy and envier, the governor of Basra, wrote to the sultan, telling him that Captain Ra'ees craved after the great wealth. Hence he left his fleet to confront the Portuguese and left with the wealth to Egypt. The Sultan ordered his governor of Egypt to arrest Ra'ees and hang him. His mistake cost him his life and his accomplishments.

Since that time, the Suez Gulf, Arab Gulf, Oman Gulf, Aden Gulf, Red Sea, and the Indian Ocean all became Ottoman's waters. Victories of the Ottoman Empire continued in these maritime routes until the Portuguese left forever.

THE ARAB GULF UNDER THE

OTTOMAN CONTROL

The Ottomans began their campaign in the east by taking over Baghdad from the Persian Safavids Dynasty. In November 30, 1534, they tried hard to strengthen their rule in Iraq and further south toward Kuwait, Al-Ahsa'a, and Nejd. When the Ottoman sultan Suleiman Al-Qanouni was still in Baghdad, the amir of Basra Rashid bin Mughamis came to him and declared loyalty to the sultan personally.

After a year, the amir sent his son Mana' and Minister Mohammed to Aderna. The sultan received them in his palace on July 24, 1538. Mana' gave the sultan the official keys of Basra. Since that date, Basra became an Ottoman governorate.

The Basra governorate included the entire southern region of Iraq, Kuwait, Al-Ahsa'a, Qatif, Najd, Qatar, Bahrain, Oman, and Shummar Mountain. The sultan appointed the Amir Rashid as the governor of Basra.

After the death of that governor, the sultan delegated Basra governorship to the governor of Baghdad Aayas Pasha[4] in addition to his duties. The sultan kept assigning both governorships to one person until they realized that the task was too much to handle by one person. Hence, the Sultan appointed Quopad Pasha and had a separate governor for Basra and another for Baghdad. Later on, Al-Ahsa'a became a separate governorate that included the region around it.

The administration of both governorates, Baghdad and Basra, were entrusted in the hands of Pashas. They were considered in the rank of ministers. They were selected from among the renowned Turkish families by the sultan himself. They were given unlimited authority as being representives of the sultan in their entities. They usually used the *gendarme*, that is, military police, against any rebels or troublemakers or simply to keep security.

However, in 1834, the sultan and his government made drastic changes in the administration of the governorate. The new governors who replaced the pashas were stripped from their authorities over the justice, finance, and security in the governorate. These were handled by departments connected directly to their counterpart's ministries in Istanbul. The governor became the administrative and political representative of the government in Istanbul. They also dealt with foreign consuls, chiefs of tribes, etc.

---

[4]   'A former title placed after the name of high official during the Ottoman Dynasty. The title was delegated by the sultan to any person who offered great administrative accomplishments. The title used to be given to the Turkish or any subject of the Ottoman Empire.

The most important job of the governor became to collect taxes. This also made the Arabs who lived under the Ottoman's rule most discontent. Tribes quite often declared their refusal to pay taxes. Besides, governorship became undesirable as being away from Istanbul instead of being an honor for a pasha to serve the sultan. The governors were overtaxing people, including continuing to use taxes that had been abolished.

One of the great problems for the governors was that they had no authority over the army or the gendarme. If the governor needed the help of the army, he had to go through the army commander, which could take some time before he got it. Besides, the gendarme who was supposed to keep up security had a triple connection: with the governor, the military commander, and the Ministry of War. Therefore, they were not easily held accountable for their malfunctions.

The governor chaired the administrative council, whose members were partly appointed by the governor, and the other part was elected by the people. This council had only advisory function and rarely met. There was a municipality council in each city. Its effectiveness was not better than the administrative council.

The Ottomans were not much better than any other invader or colonist of region or country. However, the Ottomans were more humane because of their religious and historical ties with Iraq, Arab Gulf, and Arabian Peninsula. But the situation was that some distant regions or districts witnessed injustice and oppression because of misconduct of some governors. They were violating laws and legislations, exaggerating in tax collections and treating people harshly because they were far from the center of the decision making. Many historians cited these violations of governors as the characteristics of the Ottoman occupation.

The Ottoman government enacted strict laws and policies to prevent governors or their subordinates from breaching the trust, violating laws and measurements, and/or treating people unjustly. These laws and instructions, which were called the new justice system, were to get rid of oppression and prevent the strong from taking advantage of the week. The government made its motto: "Justice is the basis to govern." In order to apply these reforms, the government initiated and/or strengthened the Justice Department, Grievance Bureau and the Supreme Bureau of Justice. The function of these institutions was to hear from people their grievances.

Therefore, it is unfair to put the Ottoman's rule of its possessions of the Arabian regions at the same footing as the Portuguese, the British, or Dutch. While the Ottomans came to save the Muslim areas and the merchant ships from the cruel treatment of the Portuguese and prevented the British from exploiting the Muslim regions as well as monopolizing trade, the other transgressors had clear ill intentions.

As we mentioned earlier, the amir of Basra Rashid bin Mughamis went to Baghdad to meet the Ottoman sultan for giving him his loyalty, making the Basra governorate part of the Ottoman Empire without a fight. This was quite unusual for a sheikh of a tribe who ruled the southern region of Iraq and up to Oman to give it up voluntarily unless he was sure that his governorate would be safer and better off under the Ottoman's rule.

When the Ottoman sultan defeated the Safavids in the famous battle Ajnadeen, which ended the Persian occupation of central Iraq; the Iraqis considered the Ottomans as saviors. The sultan showed his good intention by appointing the amir of Basra as its first governor.

How the Ottomans Dealt

with Local Sheikhs

In this section, we shall take the Basra governorate as an example. After the receipt of the official keys of Basra from the son of the amir of Basra, the sultan issued a proclamation appointing the amir as governor of Basra. During the following eight years, everything was normal. Then the governor died. His son Mana' expected to take over the governorship after his father. The sultan appointed Aayas Pasha, the governor of Baghdad, as the governor of Basra in addition to his job. This move started trouble in the area. Actually, the sultan thought that he should select the most qualified person rather than a heritage from father to son. But Mana' was thinking in terms of tribal tradition; the oldest son replaces the father as the sheikh. The delegation of Basra governorship to an Ottoman person aroused the chiefs of tribes in the southern region of Iraq. They took a stand against the Ottoman government, declaring their disobedience. We shall cite some excerpts of a letter sent by Wazeer Ali Pasha, the new governor of Basra to the sultan in Istanbul on December 2, 1701:

> Five months after your servant arrived Basra came the complainant Sheikh Mana' of the Muntifiq tribes asking for reconciliation. But, he did not enter Basra City. We arranged meeting with him in the outskirt of Basra. He accepted to be the administrator of the region which is under his control. He swore an oath on the Holey Quran that he will make the Arabian tribes to leave the islands[5] and he would administer those islands. Your servant offered him the Ottoman attires for the other chiefs of tribes and their sons to be sent to them at their tents. After he returned to his tent, he back down to what he agreed upon in return for 1500 Liras that were given to him by the Persians. He ordered to give his son Hmoud 5 islands and 3 regions. Few days later, he fell sick and returned home. When he was home, he traded his son with some regions in return for the 5 islands. They planned to take over the islands later.
>
> After the death of Mana', Mohammed Al-Fadhil declared himself as the chief of the Rashid tribe. He forced the chiefs of tribes to obey him and took over the desert. However, when the sheikhs

---

5 · *Islands* here refers to lands that are slightly above the water of the marshes in the southern region of Iraq [the translator].

of bani Lamm and Al-Hoyza tribes heard of the death of Mana', they came for the condolences. They took the opportunity of all being there, to meet. They agreed unanimously to have Hmoud the son of Mana' to be the chief. They all swore an oath to that effect.

After that, we received letters from the sheikhs of bani Lamm and the Muntifiq declaring that Hmoud was the appropriate Sheikh and they would not accept any other person. They were asking to send him the sheikhdom attire. When I requested that he should come to get it, they insisted on us to send it to him. We agreed to their demand and sent the robe of honor with his men in a very respectable way. However, they are still in the islands and regions that belong to the Ottoman Empire.

The sheikhs of the southern region of Iraq used to divide the products of dates, rice and cereals between themselves and the farmers at 50-50. Hence, there was nothing left for our Government.

Since I came to Basra until now, I tried to treat people as nice as possible to win their love and trust according to their tradition. God help me, I will never let them down, though it is very hard to deal with them. The main problem is that they are not accustomed to receive directives from a government official until recently. They became wealthy having many servants. They are not satisfied with the sheikhdom. They say this Governorate has been ours for ages. We inherited it from our ancestors, but the Ottomans took it

from us by force. Since it now in our hands, we
shall not give it up. This is in short what I wanted
to report to you about them.

This letter gives a good picture of what was happening during
three centuries of the Ottoman rule of the southern region of Iraq.
While the governors were trying to accommodate the sheikhs of
tribes, the latter were never satisfied with the way they were treated.
The governor, as we saw from the above letter, came to their terms;
they backed down on their promises. Their amir Rashid voluntarily
went to Baghdad to surrender the Basra governorate and then gave
the sultan its keys, yet the sheikhs were saying the Ottomans had
snatched their land by force. What the governor who wrote the aforementioned letter did not understand about these sheikhs was that
they only submitted to power. When they found that the governor
responded to their demands, they thought of him as a weak person.

Governor Wazeer Ali Pasha stated that his policy of treating
people nicely and adhering to the demands of the sheikhs of tribes
was according to the instructions he had received in Istanbul when
he was appointed governor of Basra. It was the Ottoman's policy of
governing the Islamic–Arab territories. Besides, the governor did not
have direct control over the army or the military police to use, so he
could use the carrot-and-stick policy.

The sheikhs misunderstood the Ottomans' intention of treating
them well and forgiving their rebellious acts. The sheikhs had antagonis-
tic reactions toward the Ottoman peaceful policy instead of supporting
it. In fact, some of those sheikhs went as far as soliciting the assistance of
foreign powers and conspiring against the Ottoman Empire.

However, the influence of the sheikhs was more effective than
the Ottoman laws and the governor's leniency. The governor's attempt
to spread welfare, security, and justice among people collided with
trouble created by the sheikhs. This situation was the same during
the Ottoman government's lethargy and apathy as when it was fully
awake and energetic.

In the year 1592, the Beni Khalid tribe took over regions that
were part of Al-Ahsa'a governorate. The sultan replaced the former

governor Yusuf Pasha with Othman Pasha. When the new governor was still in Basra, on his way to Al-Ahsa'a, thinking of a plan to combat the transgressors, he received a letter regarding the situation in Al-Ahsa'a governorate; we shall quote some of it:

> This order is directed to the Governor of Al-Ahsa'a Othman May Allah help him. The former Governor Yusuf sent a letter to His Excellency the Sultan telling us that some Arabs (bani Khalid) took over some areas part of Al-Ahsa'a Governorate. The revenues of Al-Ahsa'a before were 245,000 Liras, while the expenditure was 325,000 Liras. Now the revenues went down to 150,000 Liras. I used (that is Yusuf) whatever I had of money to construct two ships and sent them in the Gulf for observation. We were able to capture the rebellious Hassan Horaishi and 15 of his men. They were beheaded to get rid of them. In order to defeat the rebels, you should send troops. Do not delay or neglect this duty. Go to Al-Ahsa'a taking with you a tax collector. Do not spare any time in guarding the area and up keeping people's rights. According to the letter sent to you, you should spread justice and rebuild the liberated regions. Try to expand the area that belong to your Governorate and increase state revenues. You should take some of the employees from Baghdad and Basra to serve with you temporarily. They may go back to their posts later.

To sum up, there was good intention on the part of the Ottomans during their early rule of southern Iraq and its tributaries. They wanted to organize life, win people support, provide services, and renovate administrative services. They faced a stubborn rigid tribal system that opposed everything, regardless whether it was for their benefit or not. Such conflict resulted into the collapse of the reform efforts for improvement.

Section 2

World Powers Struggle for the Gulf and Arabian Peninsula

We shall discuss in this section the struggle and competition between the British and the Ottomans after the subsidence of the Dutch and the Portuguese from the region. We shall include the stand of local tribes in that struggle. The Ottomans claimed being the religious and historical custodian of the region. That was the reason for the Ottomans to enter into a long, costly war with the British over the control of the Arab Gulf and the Arabian Peninsula.

The Ottomans and the Desired World Powers

The Ottomans fought a long war with the Portuguese in the Red Sea and the Indian Ocean. Although the Ottomans did not eliminate the Portuguese from the region, they minimized their existence to the extent that they were of no danger to the commercial ships of the Muslim merchants. The other rival to them was the Persian Safavids, who were in control of central and northern Iraq. They were discriminated and marginalized, the Sunni people in their area. The Ottomans felt it was their duty to save Iraq from the aggression of the Safavids, especially because they were Sunni as the Ottomans were. Besides, the Safavids provoked the Ottomans to keep them away from finishing the job with Portuguese because Safavids sympathized with the Portuguese and had a treaty with them.

In the early seventeenth century, the Indian Ocean and the Arab Gulf played an important role in the struggle of world powers. At that time, the British entered the region after they had an alliance with the Iranian Shah Abbas the First (1557–1628).[15] That alliance drove the Portuguese from Hermes Island and the other islands at the entrance of the Gulf. The British continued to help the Iranians in their aggression on Arab areas of what is now the southern region of Iran and the eastern shore of the Arab Gulf.

The British established many commercial centers in major ports of the Gulf using the Indian Eastern Company[16] for that purpose. They were able to eliminate the competition of the Dutch and the French in the Gulf. They worked very diligently to make the Arab Gulf as a British lake. The presence of the British in the Arab Gulf had its political and military dimensions in addition to its commercial aspect.

In the year 1764, the British set up a consulate in Basra after the Indian Eastern Company had moved its commercial activities to Basra a year earlier. They also moved their warship fleet to the Gulf, claiming to protect their commercial ships. During that time, there was an influx of British who were coming in the area as tourists, researchers, or merchants. They were actually gathering information about the area and its people. They were making studies about the habits, social relations, economic conditions, etc. Some of these groups were spies, but others were commissioned to make studies in their fields. All these studies and reports were given serious attention by decision makers.

This new situation that took place in the Gulf was considered dangerous and detrimental for the southern region of the Ottoman Empire. They considered that it was their duty as Muslims to protect the people of the area. They also realized that they were in a long slumber while other powers were working continuously hard. Now they had to wake up in the second half of the nineteenth century. The British had their plan not only to kick out the Ottomans from the Gulf and the Arabian regions but also to eliminate the Ottoman Empire entirely.

THE BRITISH VERSUS THE OTTOMANS IN THE GULF

The British entered the Arab Gulf gradually and smoothly under the umbrella of commercial activities. They started by establishing headquarters for the Eastern Indian Company in Basra. Their next step was to authorize the Company as their consulate. After that, they increased their commercial fleet. They brought in warship fleet to the Gulf, claiming to protect their commercial fleet and their merchants. Historically, the British mixed their political maneuvering with military power after having studied the area and its people deeply, thus taking their time to accomplish their ultimate goal. The European powers were always in a hurry to take over and thought of themselves superior to the indigenous people by treating them harshly without thinking or even knowing about their tradition. Hence, the European colonization had its self-destructive elements in it.

Wherever the British used to go, they developed their trade and made intimate relations with the dignitaries of the area. They used to throw lavish dinners and give fancy gifts these dignitaries, especially their wives. They were paying attention to the relationship between the tribal sheikhs or religious men and their constituents. They pretended to be against the differences between the different factions of the Arabs. Yet they utilized these differences to control them all. Their motto was "divide and rule." They pretended in front of the Europeans that they were the guardians and defendants of civilization.

The British used their consulate in Boshihr to make contact with sheikhs of the regional tribes and their constituents. It was working hard to induce people to its side and accept them as friends. Their men were working in both coasts of the Gulf and its islands. They covered the area from Masqat to Basra. If the British government desired to accomplish something in the area, they would have its consulate to draw the plan and execute it because they had the knowledge of the region more than those politicians in London.

The Turkish field marshal Nassrat Pasha pointed this out in a detailed report about the British policy, which was characterized with wickedness and deception. He warned his government of their danger in the region. He said,

The British Government used to establish schools run by its Consulate claiming their intention was to spread civilization and eliminate illiteracy. They had a school in every village or city of the Ottoman Empire. It sent tourists who used to stay long period of time wandering around to write books and distribute them to people which distort Islam. These books were written in Arabic, Turkish and Kurdish languages. They tried to sway people from the authentic religion of Islam. The Consulate used to give its employees including high ranked personnel long time employment; 20–30 years in the region to gain comprehensive knowledge and make intimate friendships with leaders of the region. They were required to submit daily, weekly, monthly and annual reports which were sent to certain departments in the UK to be studied and make recommendations.

The determination of the British wicked intention and sneaky schemes can be considered more dangerous than the Russians ideology and their antagonism to our Empire. The Russians were working in the open which indicate their courage. We can counterpart their actions. But the British use deception and duping under the umbrella of justice and civilization. They do not spare any trick to accomplish their plans.

Although this warning came somewhat late, it was good enough for the Ottomans to be careful with the British, especially that it came from a high-ranked officer. In this contest, the Ottoman Deputy Consul in London confirmed the aforementioned letter of the officer. He brought an interesting point about the method that the British used in Iraq. They used to send a group of scientists in the various fields of knowledge to study the country and the people. In 1867, the British sent a high-ranking delegation to Iraq and appointed a political personality instead of a consul as they did in India. In order to protect that political person, they requested to send a military squad for that purpose. The politician was not appointed by the Ministry of Foreign Affairs but by the British Government of India . . .

Hence, the Ottoman Empire was no longer a defensive barrier to protect the region. The British came to a conclusion that they should not undertake large investment projects or bilateral trade with the Ottomans because they were backward and falling behind the new civilization as well as the principles of international trade. For these reasons, the British believed the Ottoman nation must be eliminated and torn off so that the British would control the Arabian territories and the Arab Gulf in particular.

In many books written by British about the Middle East, the authors advised the government to take over the region in all available means and ways. Mr. Curzon, the advisor of the Ministry of Foreign Affairs, wrote a book on Iran recommending that the British government should cooperate with Iran and let it expand through the Arabian territories. He also showed in his book his hatred of the Ottoman government. He urged his government to stop the Ottomans from expanding southward to control Al-Ahsa'a and down to Oman.

Besides, the British circulated rumors among the Arabian tribes that the Ottomans were taking over their territories to exploit them and limit the freedom the sheikhs used to have. They tried to convince those sheikhs that they were not in any danger of having the Ottomans conquer their area and collect taxes from them as their savior.

The Beginning of the British Infiltration in the Middle East

We have just mentioned Mr. Curzon's recommendation to his government that it should cooperate with Iran to help each other's expansion to control the Arabian lands. It should be noted that Iran was only interested in expanding its territory at the east coast of the Gulf because Iran was not a maritime nation. The British were, on the other hand, interested in the Gulf and the west coast of the Gulf. Hence, their interests were not in conflict. Besides, the British found it logical to ally with Iran, which had historical roots of antagonism with the Ottomans.

As a start, the British allowed Iran to take over Al-Ahwaz Emirate by betraying its amir sheikh, Khaz'al Al-Ka'bi. The British invited him to their ship to arrest him. They attacked Al-Ahwaz[17] to hand it to Iran. This happened at the same time when the British wanted to attack Qatar, perhaps using the same trick they had used with Sheikh Khaz'al, but Sheikh Jassim, as we noted earlier, did not fall into their trap.

The alliance between Iran and the UK goes back to the emergence of the British in the area. It should be noted that Iran during the Safavids' rule had an agreement with the Portuguese. They encouraged the latter to attack Mecca and Medina hoping that the Muslims would turn to their shrines for pilgrimage. Being a Muslim country, Iran was supposedly cooperating with its neighboring countries with which it had economic, social, and religious common denominators. But it actually was looking to dominate the Arab region at any price.

The information we have mentioned was based on letters or reports sent by persons who lived those events and observed the collaboration of the British with the Iranians as well as the intention of them. However, the Ottomans did not have qualified and experienced men to counter their enemies with plans and maneuvering policies.

A letter sent by an Ottoman spy working in the region described some events at the beginning of the British infiltration in the Arab Gulf and the Arabian Peninsula, stating, "The British tried to utilize any event to create problems in the Port of Aden, the largest port in Yemen." Some Bedouins killed the British consul and robbed a large sum of money that was with him. The British sent several warships to the port. After several hours of fighting resulted into the destruction of about one third of the city, people requested a ceasefire because they realized that they could no longer cope with the British. The latter demanded the equivalent of fifty thousand Liras as compensation. They appointed a new consul. He began immediately to practice trade and interfered in the port's affairs. He did not stop at that, but he built a house in the old wrecked castle. He also asked to have a section of the port for his ships to unload his cargoes or repair his ships. The imam (governor) of Sana'a refused the consul's request. The imam told him, "This governorate is under the sovereignty of the Ottoman sultan. May Allah support him. I am his governor, and I cannot do anything without his order." The consul replied, "This is not true. You are independent people. He kept repeating that premise over and over. However, the imam and his constituents remained firm in denying the consul's request.

But if the villagers were not supported by the Ottomans. They may have accepted the consul's desire because they were poor, and he may have bribed them with money. After the consul completed building his house and a warehouse for his merchandise in the castle, he renovated the castle to become his own fortress. The governor of Dhufar, Sheikh A'akeel, who was appointed by the sultan, had many slaves and Bedouins, but he needed a regular army from the Ottomans to support him against the British.

Logically, the respected Ottoman government should support the governorate that we are talking about to ensure that these regions will remain under its sovereignty. People will have confidence in a guardian that they can rely on. The British consul's hopes will be in vain.

The spy continued to say, "I would like to point out that the British consul asked all ship captains to raise the British flag when going to the Arab Gulf via Aden." He claimed that he wanted to know if the ship was friendly or not! All captains raised that flag whether they liked it or not. He also brought into an island soldiers to enforce his demand. He was using all kinds of tricks to show the presence and domination of the British in the Gulf.

There is a memorandum from Ali Bey[6] dated January 1888. We think it throws more light about British conduct in the region and the political situation in the Omani coast.

> After the Imam of Masqat Turki bin Sa'eed replaced his father, his brother Abdul Aziz rebelled against the new Imam. He brought with him 18,000–20,000 Bedouins to claim the Imamate. The British brought in 2 ships to bombard and dispersed the rebels. The Consul went to the Imam Turki asking him to sign a treaty with the British to protect Masqat. Imam Turki refused to sign such treaty.

> With regard to other Arab sheikhs to whom the British went asking them to sign treaties to protect them, they refused. The sheikhs usually replied that we have the Ottoman Government to resort to. They are our neighbor and share the same religion with us. Hence, they can protect us when we need that. But when Imam Turki died, he had three sons. They had an argument about who should be the next Imam? This led to a division among people. But after 3 months, they came to an agreement that Faisal would be the Imam. However, his misconduct aroused some hatred among people toward him. It is quite possible that he may lose his position for any mistake even if it is a minor one.

> The British spread rumors that Abdul Aziz, the brother of the deceased Imam, may come back to

---

6 · Bey is a title given to those who served the Empire well but not enough to deserve Pasha. People may call any person Bey for respect [Translator].

Masqat taking advantage of the dispute between Turki's sons to claim the Imamate. Hence, the British kept warship Turquoise in the Port of Masqat in case if there would be disturbance. They claimed to protect their subjects the Indian Banyan. It is known that this group were planted everywhere for the British to interfere as their protectors.

Ali Bay continues to say that even though he has not seen any political movement as far as Basra or Iraq is concerned. They are taking their time of controlling the coast of Oman and the Arab Sea step by step; the British are now dominating trade of the region. The Arab sheikhs continue to stay away from the British by refusing to sign any treaty with them. Although the British pretended to protect the Banyans, they are actually standing against any competitor as well as monitoring the tribes for any dispute to interfere and put their feet in the area. An example of the British foxy policy was that they scared Imam Faisal about the possibility that his uncle Abdul Aziz was planning to attack Masqat. Since Imam Faisal was not popular among his people, he might request British protection and sign a treaty to that effect.

To start their maneuver up north, the British got the approval of the Iranians to run their ships through the River Karun, which runs from central Iran to pour in Basra's Shatt Al-'Arab River. This would give them the monopoly of trade between Iran and Baghdad.

From these documents, we can conclude that local Arab sheikhs had their doubt in the British of justice, civilization, security, and free trade in the Arab Gulf. They knew that when they offered protection, they had many hidden conditions. Therefore, the sheikhs had to choose between British protection with its hidden conditions and the custodianship of the Ottomans under the Islamic banner. The problem was that most sheikhs were not religious adherent. Otherwise, the choice would have been easy. They used to make their calculation according to what side benefitted them more. Such a decision was taken individually, case by case, rather than collectively and consistently.

The British utilized the situation that each sheikh was independent of the other sheikhs in making his decision according to his own interest without abidance or consideration to religion, nationality, or even the affiliation to a mother tribe. The British had contacts with each sheikh to hop in when he was in jeopardy to offer their help and advice. One of the most significant differences in the struggle between the British and the Ottomans was that the former had their consul or his representative in any area could make a decision and act immediately in urgent matters then report to higher authorities because they were of high caliber. For the Ottomans, on the other hand, decision-making was in the hands of the sultan or his ministers. Even a governor whose jurisdiction extended twice the size of England had to report to his government in Istanbul about an event and wait for their answer of what to do. Such centralized administration of the Ottoman Empire, perhaps due to the fact that most governors were not highly knowledgeable nor had enough studies about the regions of the empire. The British used to spend a lot of money to send scholars making studies on every useful field of knowledge, so the consul had a huge wealth of knowledge to understand his region and could make the right decisions.

The following is another report from an Ottoman spy concerning the role of the British in the Gulf. He said that he had talked to Sheikh Mohammed bin Abdul Aziz from Qatif. The spy asked the sheikh why the Arab tribes were fighting with each other, yet they shared the same religion and heritage. The sheikh answered, "You are right in what you said. But the British got between us to create animosity to step in as protector. They are against Islam and divide the Muslims to fight with each other in order to control us. The governor of Nejd reported the fighting between us to the Ottoman government, but nothing happened."

The sheikh added, "We are not afraid of the Bahrainis. We can defeat them with five hundred men. But they are backed by the British. Where are the Cabinet members of the Ottoman government to see the transgression of the British?" The Sheikh was talking about the pain and agony among the Arab tribes. "Where is the Ottoman caliphate of Islam?"

It appears from these reports that Qatar and Qatif were not parts of the Ottoman Empire at that time. But Sheikh Mohammed bin Abdul Aziz was hoping to get some support from the Ottoman Empire, which was the greatest power of Islam. They would have accepted the support of the Ottomans even if it meant to become part of it.

* * *

CHAPTER 4

POLITICAL CONDITION PRIOR TO MIDHAT PASHA CAMPAIGN

Section 1

Late Awakening of the Ottomans

There were financial and war material supports provided by the British to the Ottomans in the latter's war with Russia in 1856 (the Crimean War). The intention of the British was by no means a friendly gesture, but for them to gain the greater share after dividing the possessions of the Ottoman Empire, which the British called the sick man without conventional war. The British support of modern weapons, ammunitions, and money to the Ottomans was a payable loan. The British had, as usual, some conditions attached to the loan; the Ottoman government should ignore any infiltration activities of the British in the Arab Gulf region. Governors should be instructed officially to abstain from provoking British personnel.

It is surprising that the Ottoman leadership would accept such a condition, which usually the British put in very vague and extendable sentences. There were so many letters and reports from various Ottoman high officials or spies, some of whom we cited in chapter 3, warning of the sneaky and tricky activities of the British. In fact, a very high-ranked army officer pointed out that the British are far more dangerous than the Russians. Perhaps there could have been a way that the British used to get such an agreement through that remained secret.

The Ottomans' neglect of the Arab Gulf region for several decades could be the application of that agreement. Besides, they were busy with some unrest in the Balkan region of east Europe. By the time the Ottomans woke up and turned back to the Arab Gulf region, the situation was completely different than before. The tribes were fighting with each other and spread all over the deserts of Yemen and Nejd. It became difficult for the Ottomans to expand or gain control into the region even after they took over Baghdad and were handed the Basra governorate. The latter included Basra, Kuwait, Bahrain, Nejd, Al-Ahsa'a, Qatar, and the coast of Oman. Such control was not continuous. There were many rebellions and civil disobedience. The Ottoman Empire sometimes extended to Masqat, but other times it subsided to Kuwait. The reasons for this situation were the neglect of the central government and the inefficiency of the governors and/or their subordinates. This situation encouraged the British to penetrate into the region and establish themselves within the society. They found out how backward the tribes and their leaders were. They were able to win many of them with gifts and lavish banquets. Yet the Ottomans were taking a long nap.

The Return of the Ottomans

In the second half of the nineteenth century, the British exposed their intention in the region by taking over Masqat and Bahrain. This action was communicated to Istanbul with a letter sent by the governor of Baghdad. However, the answer that came from the sultan on February 22, 1869, was apathetic and showed the unseriousness of the matter. The following is a part of the letter:

The transgression of foreign power over Islamic entities is unacceptable. The Ottoman would not stop before offering the sacrifice and do as much as possible to keep its possessions from any transgressor and protects its people. Normally, when a country stands ready to protect another and fulfilled its obligations, the protected region or country becomes connected to the protector. However, we see, for example, Masqat has been an independent Emirate. Its connection with our Empire was verbal talk leading to nothing.

If we talk about the Islamic World, we think it deserves our care and protection. But, the Islamic entities have not adhered to us as their religious and administrative authority. When they had problems, they come running to us. But in times of peace and prosperity, they forget us. Therefore, there is nothing to gain from any sacrifice for these regions. The case for our Empire to protect these regions and restore their rights requires spending lot of money and occupying ourselves in a matter that does not affect the Empire directly is not quite rational.

Accordingly, we think that the first order of action is to keep intact the regions under our control through improvement of their administration, providing means of development and enhance the security system. When these are accomplished, people will submit to authority. You must direct the administrators in the regions that are under our control toward this route and let it be their priority.

As far as Bahrain is concerned, it is considered
good region and it belongs to us. Its people
pay taxes to our Administrator of Nejd, Hence,
we should take wise and effective measures to
secure its people when it is necessary. We should
improve its condition and support those who are
on our side . . .

From this document, we can see clearly the new trend of the
Ottoman Empire of separating religion from politics. Perhaps the
sultan was ill-advised by some of his government who were serving foreign powers whether they knew it or not. Besides, the sultan
seemed to be naive in politics. He could not see why the British were
trying by all means to take over the Arab Gulf region. Thus they were
spending large amounts of money and manpower to gain control of
the region. If the sultan did not care to save the area from foreign
powers for religious reasons, he should think about the economic
benefits of the region which the British realized. About a year later,
the British entered the waters of Bahrain and started to mingle with
its leadership, which led to take it over. Prior to that, they controlled
Oman, which used to belong to the Ottomans.

In the beginning of 1870, the British sent four warships to
Bahrain. They removed its ruler, Sheikh Mohammed bin Khalifa,
and exiled him to Bombay. They appointed his brother Ali as the
sheikh of Bahrain. When this news got to Istanbul from the governor
of Baghdad, the government enquired from the British embassy in
Istanbul about the matters in Bahrain. The embassy replied, "Lord
Clarindon has no knowledge of this matter."

For quite some time, the Bahrain islands were a sanctuary for
pirates. Hence the British claimed that they wanted to protect their
commercial ships from the pirates. They also claimed that they did
not know Bahrain was part of the Ottoman Empire. They thought
that these islands were within the Iranian territorial waters. In his
reply to the British claims, the Ottoman ambassador in London said,

> Iran does not have any right in the Arabian Islands
> in the Arab Gulf including Islands of Bahrain,
> but they have been part of Basra Governorate
> since ancient times. When the Ottoman Empire
> controlled Baghdad and Basra, Bahrain Islands
> became consequently part of the Ottoman
> Empire.

By replacing Sheikh Mohammed with his brother Ali, the latter became their boy. This way they made sure that he would not resort to the Ottomans for protection against them. Of course, the British told the new sheikh that their warships were against the pirates and any claimant of the sheikhdom. They used the same method when they took over Masqat and the coast of Oman.

Qatar, however, remained firm against the several attempts by the British to take over it, except for paying the new sheikh of Bahrain nine thousand rials under pressure from the British. Qatar at that time was not part of the Ottoman Empire.

MIDHAT PASHA, THE NEW OTTOMAN GOVERNOR

The succession of events and their effects on the Arab Gulf region raised the political awareness focused the attention of the Ottoman government. It began to realize how great the danger around them was. Hence, the sultan appointed Midhat Pasha (1822–1884) governor of Baghdad and Basra on February 27, 1869. The selection of this man who was known for his efficiency was an indication that the government desired to enter the field of events.

Midhat Pasha

In light of this information, the Ottoman government should race against time and take appropriate measures to face the dangerous situation in the Arab Gulf region. Thus appointing a strong and wise person to the region indicated their desire to face the competition of the British, whom they used to consider their friends before.

Although Midhat Pasha was the best selection to deal with the tricks and maneuvers of the British, he was not quite familiar with the mentality of the tribal sheikhs and the social and economic conditions of the society. They had rebelled against the Ottomans even when they were strong. Besides, if showing muscles against these tribes was useful, the British would not have had to spend a great amount of money and have their best intellectuals set foot in the area.

The religious factor and the Islamic caliphate, which Midhat Pasha tried to rely on, were not sufficient to solve the problem because of the accumulation from the past of the governors' malfunctions. Most of the governors that were sent to Iraq thought that they were exiled for inefficiency. They used to collect as much as possible of wealth through overtaxation, bribery, and using their position to make money illegally. Since people usually associated the behavior of these governors and their subordinates with the government at large, the reputation of the caliph became bad. Besides, the reputation of the caliph during the reign of Sultan Mahmoud the Second reached its lowest level after the massacre was ordered by the sultan based on misleading reports from his governors. The Ottoman army attacked the holy cities of Mecca and Medina, killing a huge number of people.

The religious, political, and social conditions were so complicated that it is hard to put it in any theoretical framework or acceptable logic. Tribes used to fight another tribe for trivial matters in spite of sharing the same religion, ethnicity, and being neighbors. They often lost men and property, more than what they had fought for. Besides, when there was a battle, it would be followed by many other battles for the same reason.

It was necessary to study these problems prior to design security or justice systems as well as make programs to enhance people's living standard, provide jobs, etc. Following these steps, the chief administrator should clear old hostilities between tribes. The governor and his subordinates should solve the problems that led tribes to rebel against the Ottoman government before rushing to fight the rebels. They should follow the British model of using the carrot before the stick.

However, Midhat Pasha did not have the time for a long-term plan as the British had. He did not have the time for gradual improvement to reverse people's feelings toward the Ottoman Empire, which had its roots in the hearts of people for centuries of malfunction by administrators. History throws responsibility in both religious and moral aspects on the shoulders of the entire government, including the sultan. It is not acceptable to ignore once-greatest cities in the world—Basra, Baghdad, Mosul, and Damascus by an occupying empire which had the greatest wealth in the world. Where are the Ottomans from Omar, the second caliph after the profit (PBUH) who said, "If a mule tripped in Iraq, I will be worried that Allah will hold me responsible for not paving the road for her"? Its capital was Medina, thousands of miles away. Such neglect of the Ottomans was, for centuries, not for a short period of slumber.

THE ADVANCE SCOUTING OF THE CAMPAIGN

Although the Midhat Pasha campaign came late, it was expected to save some of the Arab Gulf and the Arabian Peninsula regions from falling in the hands of the British. Before the campaign started, it was necessary to gather information about the entire region, which showed uneasiness of the tribes for lack of security and the negligence of the Ottoman government. What came to people's minds if asked about the Ottoman government was collecting taxes, transgression on the tribes, lack of security, and ignoring foreign powers' activities. These were the reasons for some tribal sheikhs to turn to the British for support or alliance.

After he gathered detailed field information, the picture became clear for Midhat Pasha, who was the governor of Baghdad and Basra as well as the commander of the Sixth Army. He realized that he must rebuild the maritime fleet in the Arab Gulf and reconstruct the Basra shipyard basin. He wrote a letter to the sultan:

> To his Excellency the Sultan . . . This is the opinion of your servant. There is no need to repeat to your Excellency that Basra Gulf (he meant Arab Gulf) is an important part of the Indian Ocean. The shipyard basin that was established in Basra was for the Ottoman ships to travel from the Red Sea to the Arabian Sea to the Indian Ocean and finally to the Arab Gulf became completely obsolete through time.

The letter continued to tell the sultan about the old ships that should be replaced with new ones. He gave the cost of such renovation, which would be recovered and given extra revenues. However, if these ships and the shipyard were not renovated, the Ottoman

Empire would lose its vital maritime route for trade and protection of its possessions in the Arab Gulf and the Arabian Peninsula.

The crossing of the British from India to take over Aden and extended their hands to get hold of Masqat. They are thinking of controlling the Arab Gulf through interfering in the affairs of Bahrain. The Persians also claim their right over Bahrain without any acceptable legal ground. All these have been happening because the Ottomans suspended their maritime activities. People of the region have not seen the power of the Ottoman Empire to stand against foreign power interference. Hence, Arab tribes may incline toward foreign powers for protection and help. Such inclination may be reversed if the Ottomans show their strength. For example, we have noticed that people were affected when they saw our ship raising the Ottoman flag going through the Gulf.

> Accordingly, as we informed the Ministry of the Navy lately, we humbly believe if we reserve 3 or 4 small or large ships instead of the deteriorated ships (Bursa and Izmir) sending them to Istanbul before they become unable to move by themselves. Besides, we shall rebuild the Basra basin and provide it with all the necessary workshops, factories and army barracks for protection.

> In short, if the Sultan orders to write off the old ships that do not fit for operation and replacing them with the new ones which can operate from Basra to Kuwait, Bahrain and Masqat and back, they will recover the cost within short time.

> If there is an approval of this plan and appointment of qualified officers to organize the marine administration, your humble servant will cooperate with them. If we put this plan into effect, with the help of Allah, you will get its fruits in

short period of time. The decision is in you're the
hands of your Excellency.

This letter was dated March 18, 1870, and signed by Midhat
Pasha, the governor of Baghdad.

The British, on the other hand, took over Bahrain, as we mentioned before. They were coming closer to Qatar, Qatif, and Al-Ahsa'a.
If they were successful in reaching these entities, the Ottomans' rule
of Iraq and the Arabian Peninsula would come to an end after being
under their control for four centuries.

Therefore, Midhat Pasha had to move quickly, starting by sending warships and commercial ships into the Gulf waters to see the
reaction of the Arabian tribes through spies. Midhat Pasha instructed
to bring into the Red Sea and the Arab Gulf five warships to protect
the commercial ships and residents of the Arabian entities that were
under the Ottoman rule. But that fleet changed its course to go to
the Roman coast and the Mediterranean Islands because of the disturbance the Ottomans were facing. Later on, they sent two warships
to the Middle East.

The administration of Midhat Pasha began to follow up with
the reports to get as much information as possible. Midhat Pasha sent
a letter to the commander of the war fleet, asking him to send warships to the Gulf. He was advised to treat people nicely and encourage them to support the Ottomans. He had to assure them that these
ships would not harm them in any way or interfere in their disputes.
He was told to respect the chiefs of tribes. It was hoped that the tribes
would have peace and harmony among them under the banner of the
Ottoman Empire.

The Ottomans began to send commercial ships between Basra
and the Suez. The main purpose of these ships was to establish presence in the Arab Gulf through the Red Sea, rather than commercial benefits. Midhat mentioned the actual reason for sending these
ships to the Gulf in a letter dated January 4, 1870, to Istanbul, four
months before the campaign started. He said although the Arab feeling toward the Ottoman Empire had been stronger than people of
other areas because of religion, they had been neglected for too long

a time. The governors and subordinates mistreated people, had no respect to sheikhs of tribes, overburdened people in taxes, and did not offer adequate services, including security. This situation gave the British the opportunity to present themselves as protector in return for just raising the British flag on their ships. Hence, the residents of the coasts had to accept the British offer.

The Ottomans bought three ships from London. They called them *Babylon*, *Nineveh*, and *A'ashour*. They also designated a lot of funds for the reconstruction of Basra Basin and to help its workers.

The operations of SS *Babylon* and *Nineveh* brought in large amount of revenues. The third ship was sent to India after being in Boshihr Port. It was then loaded with cargo to pretend that it was going in a commercial voyage, but actually they put an inspector on board to collect information.

* * *

Section 2

Political Condition in Qatar
and Other Regions' Entities

Midhat Pasha received a great deal of information from the inspector who accompanied SS *A'ashour*. In September 1870, the ship sailed from Basra to Qatif, Qatar, Bahrain, and other ports on the Gulf. It arrived back in Basra on January 12, 1871. The Ottomans pretended that this ship was conducting commercial activities. It was carrying commodities, but the main reason for its voyage was for the inspector to gather information and make contacts with some sheikhs in the area. The inspector submitted a report to Midhat Pasha about the political, economic, and social conditions of the people in the Arab Gulf region. He also included his conversations with the British sheikh of Bahrain and many other interviews he conducted with dignitaries. Thus the report gave Midhat Pasha a comprehensive picture of the situation in the region.

Survey of Bahrain and Qatif

In his report, the inspector Mohammed Baig[7] mentioned that when their ship arrived in the Strait of Qatif, they anchored in front of the Dammam Castle. "We noticed that about forty ships belonged to Sheikh Ahmad bin Ali bin Khalifa, brother of the sheikh of Bahrain Isa. There were other sheikhs with him and about four thousand to five thousand soldiers. They blockaded Qatif."

The inspector asked Sheikh Ahmad for the reason they blockaded Qatif. He answered, "They are in war with them, so we do not want anybody to go in or out of Qatif. Besides, Bahrain confiscated all ships belong to people of Kuwait and Qatif and kept them in Bahrain."

7

The inspector said, "The sheikhs came to our ship telling us that they would not allow us to land our passengers and/or cargoes here unless the sheikh of Bahrain would approve that. They moved their ships to surround ours from all sides."

"Then I asked the sheikhs, 'Why are we besieged? Are we in war with you or are you wanting us to leave?'

"They answered that they had been blockading Qatif for five months by order of the British. 'We do not want anybody to help them or give them munitions.' They added, 'If you stay for a whole year, we shall not allow any person to come to you for munitions. Hence, it is wise for you to leave.' They also told me that they sent a letter to Mr. Doneek, the British captain in Bahrain, and that they were awaiting his instruction.

"Since there was no reply from Mr. Doneek, a letter was written to him by Sheikh Ahmad and the captain of our ship. I asked the sheikhs why they had to consult the British for every matter while Bahrain was part of the Ottoman Empire. Sheikh Ahmad answered me that we were part of the Ottoman Empire. But when the British transgressed on us, the Ottomans did not come for the rescue. Then there was dispute between my uncle Sheikh Mohammed and my father, Sheikh Ali. My uncle went to Kuwait, but my cousin Sheikh Nassir, who supported my uncle, went to Nejd to seek refuge with the Hajjar tribe. We sent a complaint to the governors about the British interference in our affairs and about my uncle, but there was no response."

"Sheikh Ahmad added that his uncle and cousin came to Qatif to lead several attacks on Bahrain's berths and dockyards using ships and soldiers from Qatif. 'They killed my father, Sheikh Ali, my brother Ibrahim, and many of our relatives and people. They also looted our country. But the British came delivering my uncle and the other sheikhs who were collaborating with him by tricking them. They invited them to their ship to intercede between the two litigants, but they arrested them, except my cousin Nassir, who did not go to the ship. The latter escaped with his family to Nejd.

"'The British deported the sheikhs whom they arrested to Bombay. They are still there in prison. They appointed my brother Sheikh Isa as the sheikh of Bahrain.'[8]

"Sheikh Ahmad added, 'We were paying *zakat* (alms) in the past to Faisal bin Abdullah, Sheikh Nejd, which was part of the Ottoman Empire, in return for his protection. When we were attacked by my uncle from Qatif, he did not come forward to help us. Therefore we went to the British to get us our rights.'

"Sheikh Ahmad and his associates kept coming to our ship. They told us that Captain Doneek was supposed to answer within twenty-four hours. But we waited three days without getting any answer. Meanwhile, our food and water was depleted. Besides, we had twenty-eight passengers from Qatif, they were anxious to go to their families. We did not know what to do. Our First Captain, who was French, had a heated argument with the sheikhs. I advised him to calm down with the help of Sheikh Ahmad because we did not want to start war between us (Ottomans) and the British. I told our captain that we would like to get out of this problem without friction. We left the Strait of Qatif the following day heading to Bahrain. I went together with the First Captain to the British Captain Doneek. We asked him for the reason he did not reply to our letter. He said that he had sent his reply on time. He added that he was surprised to learn of the number of ships and soldiers. He gave permission to send one ship with fifteen soldiers secretly to the Strait of Qatif and hide there. He added that the ship should monitor if Sheikh Nassir attempted to attack Bahrain, the soldiers of that boat would warn us. My reply was, 'If you had no idea about the matter, why did you confiscate ships that belonged to individuals from Kuwait and Qatif

---

8   ·This indicates how naive these sheikhs were. The British, perhaps, started the dispute between the two brothers, helped the legitimate sheikh, and turned secretly to encourage the fugitive sheikh to attack Bahrain. They tricked him and his collaborators by inviting them on a British ship to arrest them. They appointed Sheikh Isa to be the amir. The new sheikh would definitely be under their control. Hence, Bahrain became under their rule without war [Translator].

and keep them in a Bahrain dockyard? You also refused the requests of the owners of these ships to give them back.' The British captain denied any knowledge of such confiscated ships. He said, 'If you like, we could go tomorrow to Qatif to inquire about this matter.'

"The reader should understand that lying is forbidden in Islam and Christianity. So when say something they Therefore, he lied about his knowledge of the ships blockading Qatif and the confiscated ships. The inspector would believe him because he was not accustomed to hearing people lying. Besides, the British captain knew that such a trip to Qatif would not happen because people of Qatif hated him.

"After we heard what the British captain had to say, our First Captain and I went to meet Sheikh Isa. I asked the sheikh for the reason of the Qatif blockade and preventing our passengers to go home. He denied having anything to do with that. 'It was my brother's decision to treat you that way because he did not know who owned your ship.' The sheikh added that tomorrow, by the will of Allah, all ships would be withdrawn from the Strait of Qatif, and all the ships belong to Kuwaitis and Qatifis that were withheld would be released. I demanded that the sheikh should compensate us for the costs we incurred because of his brother's action.

"After we had gotten what we wanted, our First Captain and Captain Ahmad asked the sheikhs of Bahrain for some goats, chickens, and eggs. When Sheikh Isa noticed the confusion on me, he wondered how captains of the Ottoman Empire asked for trivial things. He sent two goats and some chicken and eggs for them. As if this was not embarrassing enough, the two captains started to fight for the gift. Each claimed it was for him. Sheikh Isa, perhaps, was comparing these captains with the sophisticated, smart British captain.

"We left Bahrain the following day toward Qatif after we got a letter from Sheikh Isa to let us pass to Qatif without delay."

A day later, I met with one of the sheikhs of Qatif, Mohammed bin Abdul Aziz, who told me the following:

"The former sheikh of Bahrain, Mohammed bin Khalifa, who escaped to Kuwait, came to Qatif intending to have reconciliation with his brother Sheikh Ali through the mediation of Sheikh Qatif.

Sheikh Mohammed bin Khalifa refused the reconciliation and stole some ships, taking them to Qatar. He collaborated with his nephew Nassir bin Mubarak to attack Bahrain. They killed two brothers of Sheikh Bahrain Ali and his son as well as many other sheikhs and people."

Before our ship arrived in Qatif in five days, the inspector said, "Sheikh Bahrain Isa, brother of Sheikh Nejd, the fugitive Saud bin Faisal, and the British Captain Doneek attacked the shipyard of Qatar. They fought with those who attacked Bahrain. They confiscated fifty horses and two hundred camels which they sent to Sheikh Nejd. This was what Sheikh Abdul Aziz told me personally."

On October 3, the inspector continued, "I met Sheikh Mohammed bin Abdul Aziz again. I asked him, 'Since you are all Muslims, why all these fighting? Isn't that forbidden in Islam?' He answered, 'You are right about what you said. But all this turmoil is from the British. They do not even hide their hatred for Islam. The British attacked the Berth of Qatif five times and confiscated several ships and burned others. Even though the imam of Nejd reported to the governor what happened to us, no one came to help us or even inquire about these incidents. I do not know if the Ottoman Cabinet had any knowledge of that. Where is their care about the Muslim entities or the dignity of the Ottoman Empire?'

Survey of Nejd and Oman

The report of the inspector continued to state, "We heard from several sheikhs and people of Qatif as they all were repeating the same as what we heard from the aforementioned sheikh. We stayed fifteen days in Qatif. During this period, October 8, the bursar of Qatif's Berth told me that Sheikh Nejd Imam Abdullah had gathered soldiers and tribesmen in order to attack Oman and Masqat. He appointed Mohammed Al-Sidairy as his representative in Oman. The sheikhs of Masqat used to pay ten thousand French Rials to Imam Nejd as *zakat*. Last year, Imam A'azzan took over Masqat, killed the representative of Nejd, and refused to pay *zakat*. After taking over

Masqat and most of Oman, A'azzan is planning to attack Bahrain. But Bahrain surrendered to the British."

When Midhat Pasha read the inspector's report, he thought of punishing those soldiers on the ship, but he remembered that Istanbul would send employees or officers who were inefficient or being punished to remote areas of the Empire. So he did not punish them. This was one of the major problems of administering the remote regions. These administrators, they were not good for their jobs. They also considered being away from their residence in Istanbul made them angry, so they took it on the people of the area they administered. They also used to take this opportunity to increase their wealth by overtaxing people. Hence, the reputation of the Empire was negatively affected because of its government's policy.

The Preparation for the Campaign

and Looking for Pretense

As we have just mentioned, that Midhat Pasha was fully informed about the situation in Nejd and the Arab Gulf. He was in a race with time to salvage that region from being detached out of the Empire as well as put an end to the British infiltration in the region. It was also necessary to find a sound and acceptable reason for the military campaign to surprise everybody.

Midhat Pasha found the reasonable ground for his campaign when Faisal bin Turki, Sheikh Nejd, and its administrator died in December 1865. The dispute between his two sons, Abdullah and Saud, for their father's succession started to divide people, thus it weakened the role of the Saudis in the region. Besides, the negligence of the Ottomans to the region encouraged the British to increase their activities to control the Arab Gulf and the Arabian Peninsula.

After the British controlled Masqat, they began to move toward invading Bahrain. Midhat Pasha sent many successive reports to his government requesting to interfere in what was happening in the Arab Gulf. He was waiting to take off in his campaign and stop the British military activities. Since Nejd considered itself part of the

Ottoman Empire, the entities Bahrain, Qatif, Qatar, and Al-Ahsa'a would be automatically within the Empire as they were parts of Nejd.

MIDHAT PASHA WARNED OF THE
ANNEX OF AL-AHSA'A TO BAHRAIN

Midhat Pasha tried as hard as he could to present the situation in the Gulf and urged them to take action, but they seemed to be apathetic about the whole matter. In one of his letters, he clearly warned them about the intention of the British to disconnect Al-Ahsa'a and Qatif from the Nejd District to annex them to Bahrain. Since the British already occupied Bahrain, all three entities would be under the British control automatically without war. These are some parts of Midhat Pasha's letter:

> We had informed you so many times that the British took over Masqat to come to Bahrain. They came to Sheikh of Bahrain Mohammed bin Khalifa and his successor to surrender Bahrain to the British to protect them. When they refused, they entered Bahrain and arrested its Sheikh and his supporters sending them to exile in Bombay. They appointed Isa as the Sheikh of Bahrain. After the death of Sheikh Faisal bin Turki, the Administrator of Nejd, and the dispute between the two sons; Abdullah and Saud for the replacement. Abdullah became the Imam and Nejd Administrator for the Ottoman. Saud withdrew to Masqat to join its former Imam A'azzan who was also against Abdullah.

> The new Imam of Nejd was trying to take over Masqat. He gathered large group. But he was unable to advance. Saud and A'azzan defeated him with the assistance of the British. It appeared

that there were 6 warships were rooming in the area close to the coasts of Masqat. The British claimed that they were assisting Saud by separating Al-Ahsa'a and Qatif from Nejd to join Bahrain so that would weaken Sheikh Nejd. But actually they wanted these two entities for themselves. If the British succeeded in their plan, Nejd would have no significance but vast desert area.

Some Iraqi tribes convinced Sheikh Nejd Abdullah to abandon his conflict with his brother Saud. They also brought in Saud in the same way. This move was good but was not sufficient to solve the problem of the region. It requires an order from the Sultan to take care of the whole problem once and for all.

The Determination of the Intervention

While Midhat Pasha kept insisting on the sultan to give permission to go ahead with his military plan, he was preparing for the campaign, but very secretly. The British, however, were able to get some information about the preparation. He made some bilateral agreements with some of the tribal sheikhs. The Ottoman prime minister, Ali Pasha, told the British ambassador in Istanbul that his government had no plan to interfere in the Arab Gulf region. The British consul in Baghdad informed his government not to worry about the subject.

Midhat Pasha sent a telegram to Istanbul telling his government that as a result of the dispute between Sheikh Nejd Abdullah and his brother Saud, the latter had assembled an army and, with help of foreigners, had taken over Qatif and Al-Ahsa'a and their adjunct areas. The troops that Sheikh Abdullah sent to fight Saud under the leadership of his brother Mohammed were defeated. "If we do not save these areas from Saud, the situation would be worse than you think."

Apparently, the government was affected by this telegram. They asked Midhat Pasha who were the foreigners that helped Saud. For the government to ask such a question indicates that they were in a deep sleep. After all those reports from Midhat Pasha about what the British were doing, they asked this naive question.

Midhat Pasha answered them with a telegram:

> The British assisted Saud. The assistance in the form of money and arms was coming from Bahrain which was under their control. We believe that we should take steps by sending army to the edges of Qatif. We have to inform the Sheikh of Nejd to prepare to cooperate so that Saud and his troops would flee from Qatif and Al-Ahsa'a.

Midhat Pasha suggested bringing two columns from Syria.

> We shall prepare 5 columns with their equipment and ammunitions. We shall use SS *Bursa* and *Nineveh*, which are in their way from London carry soldiers and other things. Since these two ships are too large to anchor near the coast, we shall use small ships and sail boats to run between these ships and the Berth. We also shall summon Sheikh Nejd to accompany the troops. We suggest asking some of the Iraqi sheikhs who are reputable and known in the region. The detailed plan shall be sent to you by mail.

ADMINISTRATIVE AND LOGISTIC MOBILIZATION

Midhat Pasha mailed the detailed plan in which he reiterated what he mentioned in his telegram. He also warned them that taking Qatif and Al-Ahsa'a by Saud with the assistance from the British would make Basra, which is 340 miles away, in danger.

We shall lose our reputation in the eyes of the Arabs. The number of soldiers in the 6th army is 9,000. With effort of the Sultan, it will be brought to 10,000. Our diligent effort in the past one and a half months let us accomplish what was expected to be done in 3 years. Since Basra Governorate is vast and the tribesmen and the bedwins are not trained militarily, it is necessary to spend lot of money and efforts to make them submissive.

Besides, the army we have now is not sufficient for the task. It should be noted that among the 16 columns, there were not engaged in wars with tribes 6 or 7 times per year. Hence, sending these columns may be defeated which would be worse than doing nothing. If it is necessary, we would use 3 columns of the vanguard and 2 columns of the infantry in addition to the 100 cavalry horsemen . . . It is necessary to select from the Iraqi tribes some renowned sheikhs and from Basra City some of its dignitaries, such as Suleiman Al-Zuhair.

There is a possibility that the British would discover about the Campaign and decide to interfere by sending their ships and other ships owned by their allied Arabs. If the enemy, Saud, did not withdraw from Qatif and Al-Ahsa'a and got the British support, it is wise to stop the Campaign instead of suffer from a defeat. We should have a highly qualified army leader with long experience. I shall do my best to carry out my duty.

* * *

CHAPTER 5

MIDHAT PASHA CAMPAIGN ADMINISTRATIVE PLAN AND MILITARY ACTIONS

SECTION 1

THE ADMINISTRATIVE PLAN

The Ottoman administration tried to mislead the British by giving them wrong information about the campaign. At the same time, they were making their preparations for it in the utmost secrecy. They want to start the campaign before the British had any chance to prepare a counter plan. Midhat Pasha gave his instruction to the army division that Nejd is very important to the Ottomans. They should enlighten people about the purpose of the campaign and its end goal.

Sheikh Nejd: The Excuse of the Campaign

The resorting of Sheikh Nejd Abdullah bin Faisal was the valuable opportunity the Ottoman government was waiting for to interfere in the region. Midhat Pasha sent a letter with a special envoy to Sheikh Abdullah to encourage him that help was on the way. Midhat Pasha sent a telegram to Istanbul telling the government that the envoy found Sheikh Abdullah in the desert alone, very pessimistic, and in a state of hopelessness. However, when he received the letter, he was revived and said that victory was coming. He then called in the Arabian tribes and started to form a group of fighters. Midhat Pasha sent to Istanbul a telegram and included Sheikh Abdullah's original letter in which he requested our help against his revolt brother. This is a summary of the telegram:

> In order to start the Campaign against Saud Bin Faisal and his followers, it is required from the Government to send 2–3 columns of soldiers on ship from Basra toward Qatif and Al-Ahsa'a. It is necessary to secure 2,000–3,000 horsemen from the Iraqi tribes of Muntifiq. We also need to rally groups from the tribes of Zubair and Kuwait. Thence, we will be able to salvage the areas which were taken by Saud from his brother Sheikh Abdullah of Nejd. The man who came from Sheikh Abdullah is in Basra is asking for a definite and quick answer. If we act as planned and establish an administration, we can assist Qatif and Al-Ahsa'a that revenues of 200,000 Rials. It should be known that spring season will end in two months.

This indicates that the costs of this campaign would be recovered soon. This shows that Midhat Pasha based his plan on realistic studies and accurate information about the region. Midhat Pasha sent several communications to Istanbul with respect to the social and political situation of the region. He based that on the comprehensive reports he received from field studies sent to him by spies. He sent the following telegram to the government in Istanbul:

> According to the interest of Nejd and in response to the desire of the Sultan, we have taken the necessary precaution. Since the messenger of Sheikh Abdullah was in a hurry and also spring season ends in April after that it becomes very hot. Therefore, we sent 4 columns infantry under the leadership of Nafith Pasha. They were accompanied with horsemen and officers with their equipment. All this army was sent by sea toward Qatif. We also corresponded with sheikhs from Shummar Mountain, Anza, Barida and O'naiza in order to join the aforementioned army. We also asked the Sheikhs of Muntifiq and Zubair and some Islamic religion sheikhs to accompany the army. At the end of the Campaign, Sheikh Abdullah bin Faisal will appoint chief administrators for Qatif, Al-Ahsa'a and Qatar. We shall leave a ship with a column of soldiers in a military barrack which shall be erected there.

After reviewing the suggestions presented by Midhat Pasha, the sultan decided to go ahead with this proposal and issued the following memorandum:

> This memorandum was submitted to us (the Sultan) with the letter sent before. We have studied the plan and decided to give the permission for the arrangement undertaken by the Governor and affect all the necessary details in accordance with the instruction of the Sultan. All letters are sent back to their origin.

The period during which Sultan Abdul Aziz ruled was crowded with significant international events such as the Crimean War, the British infiltration in the Arab Gulf, etc. It was necessary to undertake political and military actions to restore the balance toward the Ottoman Empire. Among the measures to combat with these problems was the appointment of Midhat Pasha, the strong personality, as governor of Baghdad and Basra.

The appointment of Midhat Pasha was to fill in the political and administrative vacuum in the Arab Gulf region, which became a hot spot with the presence of the British. The latter entered into the dispute between Abdullah and his brother Saud for the succession of their father, Faisal, former sheikh of Nejd. After the British controlled coast of Oman and took over Bahrain, their mouth watered for Qatif and Al-Ahsa'a and beyond. Hence, they not only encouraged Saud to claim the sheikhdom of Nejd but also backed him with their warships and those of the sheikh of Bahrain, whom they appointed and controlled. Their plan was that when Saud took over Qatif and Al-Ahsa'a, which would be practically under their control, the road toward Qatar and the Arabian Peninsula would become paved for them.

All these events and conspiracies were going on while the Ottoman government was in a slumber, and their hands were tied because of the large debt from the British to finance the war against Russia. Besides, the Ottomans bought large ships from the British to fight them with! The policy of the Ottomans was that when a region that gives them high revenues was in danger, they rushed to protect it. Yet they used to neglect others of low yields. They did not think why the British tried to secure their control on these regions neglected by the Ottomans.

After the approval of the plan and the issuance of its details by the high-ranked government, the military and administrative arms began to move in the battlefield. A few weeks passed which were full of activities until the middle of April. A decision came of the appointment of Lieutenant General Nafith Pasha as the commander of the army. According to the instructions of the government, Midhat Pasha would devise his administrative and military plans as follows:

ARTICLE ONE

Commander Nafith Pasha will take the soldiers and employees as well as enough equipment, munitions, and food supplies from Basra toward Qatif coast by ships and sailing boats. On the other hand, Sheikh Abdullah bin Faisal will be given enough time to move his tribesmen fighters from Riyadh and Hafr Albatin. The administrator of Kuwait will be waiting to move by land and sea to join the other two groups. There will be a mailman to carry letters between these groups and Basra to synchronize their movements.

ARTICLE TWO

Before the departure of the soldiers, there should be training camp secured with barriers and protected by cannons from the sea. Soldiers will be trained on military techniques and instructed about the expected field operations.

ARTICLE THREE

There is a possibility that when our army arrives, Saud may flee from Qatif and Al-Ahsa'a. If this happens, he should be chased by horsemen of the tribes. The soldiers will take over Qatif and Al-Ahsa'a then advance to Qatar to become part of the Empire. Meanwhile, there will be distribution of flyers and printed materials to the entire region.

ARTICLE FOUR

Whether Saud escapes or stays to fight, our striking force should enter Qatif and Al-Ahsa'a. But it is necessary to use the utmost caution in depending on the Arabs, especially residents of the region. Therefore, before entering Qatif, there should be some communications with sheikhs of the region, giving them respect and dignity. They will be asked to assist sheikhs who came with the campaign from Iraq. There should be some soldiers assigned to go into Qatif to bring with them chiefs in order to keep them as guests in the army barrack without telling them why they are there.

ARTICLE FIVE

As indicated by the instructions of the sultan, it is not allowed to transgress on Bahrain. If Saud flees there by himself or with his followers, we should chase him until the coast of Bahrain without entering it.[18]

ARTICLE SIX

The main goal of this military campaign was to secure the administration of Abdullah bin Faisal. He should establish his district and become part of the Ottoman Empire, similar to the Administration of Muntifiq[19] (northwest of Basra). A military barrack shall be erected to house two columns of soldiers for some time. The site of the barrack should be near the coast where there is sweat water with moderate weather. It shall house the commander too. Sheikh Abdullah should be told the plan step by step so that he can carry on his duties. All sheikhs involved in the campaign shall be given fancy attire.

ARTICLE SEVEN

At the end of the campaign, the title of Abdullah bin Faisal shall be changed from district administrator to provincial governor. He will select district administrator for each of Qatif, Al-Ahsa'a, and Qatar. He will give the title of director to the sheikh of every small entity. If the Arab rejected these titles, Abdullah will remain district administrator, while the administrators of Qatif, Al-Ahsa'a, and Qatar will be directors. Sheikh Abdullah will select two deputies for Riyadh and Qasseem to represent the Hanbali sect. They should show their credentials for qualification.

ARTICLE EIGHT

Abdullah bin Faisal is committed to pay in silver money for his support to cover the expenses of the campaign. He is not allowed to collect such money from people of Qatif, Al-Ahsa'a, and Qatar. But the money should all be from his savings. He should be informed of this decision.[20]

ARTICLE NINE

Given the existing situation, it is possible that when the army enters these urban areas, it may arouse some worry and fear that the Ottomans will confiscate their properties, impose taxes, recruit their men for the army, and so on. These may be spread as rumors by the enemy. Therefore, it is necessary to invite their sheikhs to assure them that these things will by no means happen. These sheikhs should convince their fellow tribesmen to that effect. People must be told that the main goal of the campaign is to protect them rather than take advantage of them. When the campaign is over and the situation gets back to normal, the Ottoman will apply the Islamic law of collecting *zakat* from the rich.

ARTICLE TEN

Since part of the army will remain in the region, there is a possibility that some people of Bahrain may request protection. If we respond positively to them and attack Bahrain, that will bring us unnecessary headache. Besides, if Saud and his followers flee to Bahrain, there is a possibility that people of Bahrain will divide among themselves about Saud. In order to avoid that, the sultan will hasten to issue a pardon giving Saud and his followers the amnesty. This will be sent to Saud in some appropriate way. Then Saud and his followers will leave Bahrain. Thence, people of Bahrain will be protected in a general way. There should be some agents from the Bahrainis to arrange for such protection. It is advisable that Brigadier General Hamdi Pasha, who is the expert in dealing with foreigners, lead the discussion. We should be very careful not to do something that makes the British complain.

Article Eleven

There is no need to give the cavalry that are with army who will attack the Arab violators or dissidents any assistance. But the cavalry from Anza and Muntifiq, who wait for the army in the north of Kuwait, should be given assistance with fodder for seven hundred to eight hundred animals. There should be rice sent to the chiefs of tribes.

Article Twelve

The soldiers must show kindness and be just. These are the principles of the sultan. They should not transgress or transcend over any individual's rights, no matter how insignificant he is. The commander of the army must make sure of the application of this order. If the soldiers need to purchase foodstuff or their needs from any place, they should pay for it. They are not allowed to accept any gift or take things for free. These places are more in need for charity than the soldiers.

Article Thirteen

It is known that there is no communication center in these regions. Therefore, there is no way of getting the news of the events. It is necessary to send a small boat weekly with the information to the nearest center of communication. Besides, there should be a mailman that went through Kuwait to carry the news by land. If there is something very urgent and there is no small ship, SS *Bursa* to go to Boshihr. If the weather is good, you should use sailboats to dispatch the news weekly without interruption. It is also necessary to get maps of Qatif and Al-Ahsa'a and have the marine officers determine precisely the tide movement.

ARTICLE FOURTEEN

We pray to Allah that this campaign will end in the best way and to the interest of the sultan. When it is time to return, the military barrack would be erected to house two columns: vanguard and infantry. There will have their animals, guns, cannons, and the necessary foodstuff and money. Since SS *Bursa* will stay in the region, the rest of the army will be carried by other ships and sailboats. The ship SS *Khojabi* and some small ships will also remain in the region.

ARTICLE FIFTEEN

The campaign is limited and defined by the instructions stated above. But the branching activities would be decided as they come along. The commander is known for his shrewdness, and by the Grace of Allah then the support of the Sultan, everything will be fine. There is no need for more details.

The following are some comments on these instructions:

- Qatar is the final destination of the military campaign. It should become part of the Ottoman Empire as part of the plan. This indicates that Sheikh Jassim Al-Thani anticipated that. Hence, he moved ahead of the plan by inviting the campaign to Qatar voluntarily to become part of the Ottoman Empire.
- Making use of the sheikhs of Iraqi tribes to accompany the army. This was to get local people accept the campaign. Such decision gave people of the region that the campaign was not Ottomans versus Arabs.
- It was decided that Bahrain was ruled by the British was de facto, although it has been under the rule of the Ottomans for several centuries. This was to avoid direct confrontation with the British.
- The Ottomans realized, though at a late time, that their policies were not appropriate in the Arab entities. This led to disloyalty of the Arabian tribes and recurrent revolt or

disobedience. Thus the instructions were to be nice and treat the Arabs with respect. Hence this policy reversed the attitude of the Arabs toward the Ottomans and led to security and let the people of Bahrain think of requesting from the Ottomans to protect them.

- Undoubtedly, the instructions of Article 12 were from the Sultan Abdul Aziz as it was expected of him. He made them clear to the people of Nejd and its surroundings in order to assure them that they feared none from the campaign. He acted as the caliph of the Muslims. This part of his Empire, as every other one, was put under his custody by the grace of Allah. Therefore, he had to carry out his duty as custodial of the entire Empire.

- These instructions overlooked the fact that the Ottomans had choice of two alternatives: first, was to dispatch troops to restore the control of Qatif and Al-Ahsa'a by force to Abdullah, or second mediate between the two brothers to settle the dispute so that everything would go back to normal peacefully. However, Midhat Pasha drove his government for the campaign because he wanted to bring together the Arabs under the Ottoman banner and show muscles as long as the cost of the war would be paid by Abdullah, Sheikh of Nejd.

- While it was stated that the army should fulfill its promise to Sheikh Abdullah bin Faisal by returning the territories taken by his brother Saud, it did not prepare any plan if the British interfered in support of Saud. It left that for the commander to react appropriately. There was a possibility to work on a deal with the British in time.

PROCLAMATION OF THE SULTAN TO PEOPLE OF NEJD AND ADJUNCT REGIONS

As part of the plan of the campaign, it was necessary to inform residents of Nejd, Qatif, Al-Ahsa'a, and Qatar about the goal of the campaign and the intention of the Ottoman army being in the region. People of the region should not be alarmed or scared of the operations. They should reject any rumors being spread by the enemy to distort the image of the Ottoman Empire. Hence, leaflets and printed materials shall be widely distributed to people of the region carrying the title "Proclamation to People of Nejd and Its Surrounding Regions."

Oh, you people and tribes of Al-Ahsa'a, Qatif and Nejd—as you know, Nejd and its adjuncts as well as Iraq, Yemen, Egypt, Tunisia, Tripoli, and the two Sacred Cities are all belong to the Ottoman Empire. All these areas and their residents are under the protection and the sovereignty of the custodian of the two holy shrines: the Sultan Abdul Aziz Khan, the head of the Supreme Islamic Empire.

As you may have heard from your fathers and grandfathers that the previous sultans—may Allah bless their souls—were concerned with protecting residents of these regions. The Muslim Caliph considers this as his sacred duty, which needs no further explanation.

The Ottoman Supreme Government has been busy in preserving the Islamic power and protecting it for several centuries. However, when there is some unrest in the other parts of the Empire, it perhaps pays less attention to these regions as it should. Therefore, during these periods, some chaos among the Arabian tribes in the deserts of Yemen and Nejd occurs. It is regrettable to have a dispute among Muslims that developed into a fight. According to the verse 10 of chapter 49 of the Quran, "The believers are nothing else than brothers [in Islamic religion]. So make reconciliation between your brothers, and fear Allah, that you may receive mercy." And the meaning of what the Prophet said, "The faithful person to the other faithful like a tightly compacted structure, each part holds on to the other." According to the verse and the statement of the Prophet, Muslims should be united with each other rather than fight one another for personal reason and worldly benefits.

The strong person transgresses over the weak one to destroy him. What happened between Muslims was sad. It is just like what happens between strong beasts that devours small creatures. If people forgive each other, things would not be as they were. But the sultan is the protector of religion and people as it is in the meaning of the Prophet, saying, "The Sultan is the representative of Allah on earth, thus the oppressed should resort to him." And the Prophet also said what it means: "Everybody is a guardian, and he is responsible about his subjects."

Accordingly, the Ottoman government should prevent any destruction, which is contrary to Islamic religion, as brought in by the Prophet. If something happens to the nation of Islam as a result of dispute, the government should step in because the nation is entrusted in the hands of the caliph.

All laws and regulations of the Ottoman government are based on Islamic jurisprudence. It guides people to the right path to be successful and happy. It sent employees to remote areas to participate in applying justice. The intention of the government has been to spread peace and happiness. It has been like a father taking care of his children through advice to keep them on the right path to achieve success.

Those who listened to the advice and accepted it will correct their lives and arrive at their goal of happiness. They become what this verse 48 of chapter 6 describes them as: "So whosoever believes and does righteous good deeds, upon such shall come no fear, nor shall they grieve." While those who live in remote areas are in a nomadic state and ignorant, they do not realize the values of these bounties. Instead, they do not mind harming other people and continue that way until they become what this verse 95 of chapter 12 describes: "By Allah! Certainly, you are in your old error." Hence, they rebelled against the Empire, which brought them disaster. They did not follow what verse 59 of chapter 4 says, "O you who believe! Obey Allah and obey his Messenger and those of you (Muslims) who are in authority . . ." ordered them to do.

An example of this behavior was what Saud bin Faisal did. He deceived people against his brother and harmed people of Qatif and Al-Ahsa'a by attacking them. These two actions are considered the worst things to do. He transgressed over rights of the legitimate chief administrator of Nejd, who was appointed by His Excellency the Sultan. His other action was to instigate people and encourage them to be against the Ottoman Empire. He also caused division between the Muslim nations.

These actions are not acceptable by the imam of the believers, the caliph. The rights of the government were entrusted in the hands of Abdullah bin Faisal; he had to protect them. Besides, the caliph had to ensure security and order in this region as verse 7 of chapter 47 says, "O you who believe! If you help [in the cause of] Allah, He will help you, and make your foothold firm." According to this verse, we have prepared a military division from Baghdad under the leadership of Nafith Pasha. The latter led his army by ships and sailboats to the coasts of Qatif. You all should know Abdullah bin Faisal, who was appointed the head of Nejd and its adjunct regions by the respected caliph. The district administration of Nejd is attached to the Governorate of Baghdad. The purpose of keeping soldiers in the region is to ensure the government rights and preserve justice and mercy as being the moral preference of the sultan. This should encompass the young and old, men and women, rich and poor. We are all, thanks to Allah, belonging to Islam, and the caliph is our protector. He is known to have graceful treatment and concern about people regardless of their color and affiliation. The law of justice is based on the Islamic jurisprudence.

Therefore, since Saud bin Faisal is being accused of misconduct, if he regrets his action, the military division will send him to Baghdad. There will be a plea for him to the sultan to forgive him and issue for his pardon. This is in accordance with verse 9 of chapter 49: "And if two parties or groups among the believers fall into fighting, then makes peace between them both." But if he refuses and insists, he will be punished. We shall use the utmost force against him and those who will be on his side as it is clear from verse 46 of chapter 41: "Whosoever does righteous good deeds, it is for (the benefit of) his own self, and whosoever does evil, it is against his own self, and your Lord is not at all unjust to (His) slaves."

The residents of Qatif and Al-Ahsa'a, as well as those who were with the military division, if they did not rebel or disobey the orders of the officers, would have the amnesty as long as they stayed like that. Their souls, properties, and honor are protected against any person or entity. "Our prayer is to Allah to look after the Muslims from any calamity or wrong doing, Amin."

From looking at this circular proclamation, we may have the following comments:

- The proclamation indicates great legal and administrative commitments to the people of the region by the Ottoman government.
- There is an admission of the failure of former administrators during the past decades, which led to the loss of Bahrain and other territories. The governors and their subordinates were inefficient, looking for their own interests and having no idea of how to deal with Arabian tribes.
- The proclamation was too long for the tribesmen to grasp. There are so many repetitions and citations from the Quran that are unnecessary.
- It has so much praise and commendations for the sultan. It's supposed to be issued from him, yet it is repeated several times that the sultan is nice. Even Prophet Mohammed used to ask people not to praise him personally.
- It includes the resort of the Ottoman Empire for the help of Arabian tribesmen and sheikhs of the region and Iraq. This makes the Arabs partners with the Ottomans in recovering the loss of territories rather than the Ottomans being invaders for their own interests.

* * *

Section 2

Military Field Operations

Entering Nejd

It seems that the operation room in Istanbul regained its vitality as it followed up with the reports regarding the preparations for the campaign. There were five columns made, ready to form a military division whose commander was Lieutenant General Nafith Pasha; three columns to be sent to Basra led by Major General Humdi Pasha and two columns to go from Baghdad. The division will leave Basra by sea to the coasts of Qatif.

The difficult part of the plan was to send soldiers on land because they may be attacked by tribesmen on the way. There was another problem regarding the division going by sea that it should be synchronized with the tide movement to be able to anchor at the Gulf coasts and being protected by artillery.

It was estimated that the distance between anchorage of the warships and the coast was two hours. The brother of the amir of Kuwait with his infantry company and the cavalry from Anza tribe were to go by land for the protection of the division at the point where the soldiers leave land to sea.

It should be pointed out that British troops might interfere. Colonel Baily was the British resident in Boshihr and in charge of the British interests in Nejd, Masqat, and the coast of Oman. He sent three warships to the region. They anchored between Bahrain and Qatif. They were thinking of the possibility of attacking Bahrain and the outskirts of Oman. Actually, the British government of India requested through its consul in Baghdad some explanations from Midhat Pasha and an assurance about such attacks. Orders and clear instructions were given to the commander of the division to that effect.

The preparations went on as were originally planned. The division moved, crossing Kuwait. They went on ships for four days when they arrived at Ras Tennoura, which is on the coast of Qatif. But because of the bad weather, the amir of Kuwait, Abdullah Al-Sabah, could not make it on time with his ships. His brother Mubarak Al-Sabah and the cavalry of Anza could not go through on land because the tribe of Muttair blocked their way. There is no reliable source indicating why they did so.

ENTERING QATIF

Later on, the army found it possible to land. The division sent an exploratory group to the region. As soon as the news of the division got to the tribes and other followers of Saud, they began to weaken and break down. Most of those who were with Saud left, except Ajman tribesmen who were getting ready to leave to Bahrain. The commander of the division, Nafith Pasha, sent a letter to Midhat Pasha on May 31, 1871; he mentioned,

> Your Excellency Midhat Pasha. As I mentioned in an earlier telegram, I shall send you a detailed letter about the fortress of Qatif. The Amir of Qatif sent an envoy, upon the request of Saud. We sent Mohammed Sa'eed (the head of nobility in Basra) with a group of soldiers to the fortress of Qatif. They met with the appointed Amir by Saud, Abdul Aziz Al-Sidairy. The latter said that Saud treated him as gentleman and was very generous to me. I now become like a slave to him. He gave me the fortress without fight. Hence, I shall not give it to the Ottomans without fight, because it will be shame on me and the Arabs will look down to me.

> Mohammed Sa'eed presented the situation to us that they are ready to fight. But he guessed that

they want to give and take to gain some time during which they want to find out the strength of our troops and get reinforcement from Saud. Mr. Sa'eed mentioned that the fortress is very strong. It will not be easy to come close to it without losses. There are about 400 fighters inside.

In the following day, we made exploration of the roads to the fortress. We found an easy way of getting carts driven by oxen to the fortress. We sent Major Rajab with an exploratory battalion and his column. They went to the market place which is outside the fortress. When the enemy saw them, they started to shoot bullets from their rifles. This did not scare the Major or his company. They kept going with their exploration around the fortress. They ordered the nearby villagers to demolish the castles which are on the roads. The Major also ordered people to widen the bridges in the farms so that cannons can pass through. They returned to the army camp.

At that night, we sent 2 infantry columns with 2 cannons under the leadership of Major General Hamdi Pasha. He was accompanied by Mohammed Sa'eed. When they arrived to the villages surrounding the fortress, they saw armed people at the top of the observatory tower of the fortress. They were fully alert. Hamdi Pasha, at the advice of Mr. Sa'eed, brought the mayor of the village to warn the people that the Ottoman army is coming. Hamdi Pasha ordered the villagers to bring 20-30 donkeys and a guide. When it was night, they sent the donkeys to the fortress. The enemy starts shooting bullets and bombs. But the Ottoman soldiers were too far for the fire to reach them. Besides, the soldiers used the walls and houses as shelters. The army sent 2 bombs to the fortress. They began to erect barriers in the market place.

There were some more bombs sent from the fortress. Our soldiers with cannons arrived near the fortress. The Amir of Kuwait with about 100 warships and SS. A'ashour that carrying cannon also arrived to the coast of Qatif. We found that it was difficult to approach the fortress from the side where there were farms. We sent several messages to Al-Sidairy to surrender the fortress, but he refused to do so. We asked him to send civilians, especially children and elderly, out of the fortress so that they will not be in danger. When he continued to fire, we reciprocated by firing until the tower of the fortress was damaged. We then saw a white flag was raised. Hence we stopped firing. We gave them 2 hours of grace period, and then we sent Mohammed Sa'eed and Amir Kuwait Abdulla Al-Sabah to negotiate with them the surrender of the fortress.

After 2 hours, Abdul Aziz Al-Sidairy came out very depressed accompanied by his brother Abdullah. There was intercession from some dignitaries, we gave them amnesty. Hamdi Pasha and the rest of the army entered the fortress proudly. They all made supplication to the Sultan and fired 21 bombs for victory. The flag of the Ottomans was raised in the fortress. They also released men who were imprisoned by Al-Sidairy. We returned the arms and ammunitions which were confiscated by Al-Sidairy to their rightful owners. Finally, we ordered to tabulate the cannons, rifles and ammunitions and recorded that. We kept them in guarded storage.

The Ottomans suffered 2 injuries which recovered soon. The other side suffered 25 casualties. The fortress suffered from great damage. Thanks to Allah, the fortress and the rest of Qatif fell in the hands of the Ottoman army without any losses. Life got back to normal as people went back to their business as usual. On Friday, soldiers and people went to the Mosque to listen to the sermon delivered by the Imam of the army. A Provisional Council was selected to be chaired by Mohammed bin Faisal to run the District until the arrival of Abdullah bin Faisal from Nejd.

Entering Al-Ahsa'a

Following the success of the military operations in Qatif, it was taken as the center for the army in the region. A column was left in the fortress of Qatif. The army sent two infantry columns and four cannons toward the fortress of Dammam under the leadership of Hamdi Pasha. It should be noted that Mohammed bin Faisal, the brother of the administrator of Nejd, was imprisoned there. In about one hour from Qatif, the army was shot at with cannon and rifles from the fortress of O'noq. The Ottoman soldiers did not respond but stayed behind barriers. After that, someone sent a letter asking for amnesty. We gave them the amnesty and informed the commander of that. The commander made a tour around O'noq Fortress.

When the soldiers went into the fortress, they seized three cannons, ammunitions, and rifles. After they received the fortress' keys, they left a company led by Major Ibrahim at the fortress. The rest of the army went on toward Dammam.

THE WITHDRAWAL OF SAUD BIN FAISAL

When Saud saw the victorious operations of the Ottomans, he withdrew from the fortress of Dammam. He felt that we are advancing toward his place. A warning was sent to him to surrender the fortress and release his brother Mohammed. If he became stubborn and refused our suggestion, we shall take over the fortress in a few hours by the grace of Allah, as we did with Qatif.

We sent a letter to Tahnoon, who was appointed by Saud in charge of Dammam. We told him he should anticipate how many losses of lives his people will suffer. He should look at what happened to Qatif. He answered, "If you really took over Qatif, I would like to see Abdul Aziz Al-Sidairy or his brother show me an assurance that they surrendered the fortress of Qatif. In this case, I shall surrender our fortress without resistance." The reason for him not knowing about the surrender of Qatif was that it had happened one day before. Hence, the news had not reached Tahnoon.

During that night, we sent a man to bring Abdullah because Abdul Aziz was too sad to go. After Abdullah assured Tahnoon that his brother surrendered the fortress of Qatif, he came out with the keys of the fortress, and they released Mohammed bin Faisal. Tahnoon asked us to give him amnesty for the people in the fortress before we could go in.

We gave him a document that the people of Dammam and their properties are safe. The soldiers entered the fortress and found eleven cannons and a large quantity of ammunitions, which was recorded, and left soldiers to guard the storage and the fortress. The rest of the army went back to Qatif, taking with them Mohammed.

Thereafter, all villages on the coasts of Qatif came to declare their allegiance and submission to the Ottoman Empire. Hence, they avoided any problem and continued to live a normal life. Soldiers and civilians with the army were told to pay for their purchases and treat local people nicely. Officers and dignitaries with the army were asked to exchange invitations with local merchants and dignitaries to establish good relations with them and explain that they were instructed to help people rather than take advantage of them.

It was decided to go to Al-Ahsa'a. They put up their tents in place called Jaroodia where there is river water. A letter was sent to the amir of Al-Ahsa'a, who was appointed by Saud. Several letters were sent to merchants and other dignitaries there, advising them to surrender.

The commander of the division, Nafith Pasha, wrote to Istanbul from his camp in Jaroodia, saying,

> All preparations were set to go to Al-Ahsa'a. We exceeded what Abdullah bin Faisal requested from us. He wanted us to send few columns to the region to scare his brother Saud, and then return back. But to drive away Saud and his followers from Qatif, Dammam and all surrounding regions, this was beyond his expectations. Besides, according to our correspondence with him, he agreed to participate with his men in the military operations. However, while our troops were combing the region, he was still in Riyadh.

There, documents indicate that both Midhat Pasha and Nafith Pasha wrote several letters to Abdullah bin Faisal. He never replied but gave unacceptable excuses. Since he did not come to the division, they thought of sending a group of soldiers to bring him. They even thought that he perhaps had an agreement with his brother Saud to join forces to attack the Ottoman army. He, finally, found out that there was no place for him to hide. Hence, he came to the division.

Midhat Pasha wanted to meet with Abdullah to avoid breaking the promise made to him before the campaign. So when Abdullah came to the division, he was received with great respect as the district administrator. Besides, he and his brother Mohammed and their followers were given daily supplies. It was decided that his monthly salary will be 1,200 rials.

When Abdullah appeared in the division in that way, his brother Saud was enraged. In response to that, Saud prepared ten thousand fighters from the tribes of O'jman and Murra and other tribes to fight the Ottoman division.

The forces of Saud met with two columns from the Ottomans in a village near Al-Ahsa'a. The battle ended with Saud's forces losing about six hundred casualties, and he fled to Qatar. Midhat Pasha praised Saud's courage, bravery, and determination. He was able to gather troops even after his losses. He gained his reputation with the Arabian tribes.

In his visit to the division, Abdullah congratulated the army for the accomplishments and praised the soldiers' bravery. He also sent a letter to Baghdad to show his pleasure for the victory over Saud, his indebtedness to the Ottoman army. After that, Abdullah went back to Riyadh, taking with him his brother Mohammed and his followers.

When Abdullah arrived in Riyadh, he sent a letter to Nafith Pasha indicating that the government of Baghdad had declared the family of Faisal cannot become district administrator. Now, after the Ottoman army drove out Saud and the adjustment of the district became in favor of him (Abdullah), I asked the Ottoman army to withdraw their forces from the region. Since the army did not leave the region, I had to return to Riyadh. I shall continue to obey the orders of the supreme government and abide by its instructions as a follower of the government.

With regard to the declaration of Midhat Pasha in Baghdad about the family of Faisal; he had not meant to fire Abdullah bin Faisal from his job as district administrator. It was due to the complaining of people of Qatif, Al-Ahsa'a, and Qatar about their tyranny and oppression. Hence, Abdullah should be satisfied with his jurisdiction of Riyadh and its surroundings. However, he was called in to Al-Ahsa'a and given fifteen days to appear there. If he came in within that period, he would be appointed district administrator to be included with Nejd, Al-Ahsa'a, Qatif, and Qatar as it had been before. But if he did not show up on time, he would be relieved from his duty because he refused the job by himself. He was informed with that in a letter dispatched to him.

In fact, the Ottomans were very sure that he would not come on time. So it became evidence that he relinquished his right of being district administrator. He actually did not go to Al-Ahsa'a. He asked the Ottomans in a previous letter that if his district did not include the entire region as before, they can appoint someone else for the job. The Ottomans created a new district with its headquarters in Al-Ahsa'a to include Haffoof, Mabriz, Qatif, and Qatar. The commander of the division was appointed its administrator in addition to his military duty. His salary was fifteen rials. As for the other parts of Nejd, it was decided to be taken care of later.

COMMENTS ON THE PREVIOUS DOCUMENTS

According to the aforementioned documents, we have the following comments:

The campaign ended as it was planned by Midhat Pasha successfully with no losses of life.

Soldiers, officers, and Arabian tribes showed the utmost military discipline. There was no transgression on local people, their properties or honor. They treated them in a brotherly fashion. They prayed on Fridays together.

The campaign indicated changes in the Ottomans' policy toward the Arabs. They emphasized their adherence to the religion of Islam, following the instruction of Sultan Abdul Aziz.

It was unfortunate to have a dispute between two brothers that led to a fight between two sides of the Arabs and Muslims.

It was amazing that the campaign had been planned, prepared for, and executed without the knowledge of the British. The latter had intelligence and spies everywhere, but they had no clear idea of what the Ottomans were doing. This showed discipline and loyalty to the Empire.

* * *

CHAPTER 6

POLITICAL CONDITION IN QATAR

Section 1

Political Condition before
Sheikh Jassim Rule

Sheikh Jassim was observing the chaotic political condition in the Arab Gulf and the Arabian Peninsula. The dispute between the sons of Faisal and the campaign that ended the Nejd situation caused many deaths and destruction. Another event that had great impact on the region was the British invasion of Bahrain and changing its ruler to appoint Isa bin Ali Al-Khalifa, who became subservient to the British. The latter had their eyes on Qatar to be next after Oman, Masqat, and Bahrain. Besides, the British and the Bahrainis took the side of Saud and helped him to invade Al-Ahsa'a, Qatif, Dammam, and other coastal areas. They wanted to set foot in the Arab Gulf west coast. But Abdullah, as we explained earlier, resorted to the help of the Ottomans.

All these events took place, but Qatar stayed away from the events except observing them. However, Qatar was not safe from the struggle because no one can tell what the British planned to do. The northern region of Qatar was threatened by Bahrain and the southern region from Abu Dhabi, which was under the British control. The tribes of Qatar were swaying in their allegiance, which threatened its unity. At the end of 1867, the cities of Doha and Wekra were leveled to the ground. All their houses were demolished, and their residents fled for their lives. Losses were estimated at two hundred thousand rupees, which was a huge amount at that time. These two cities were the largest in Qatar. This event happened as a result of treacherous and destructive attacks by Sheikh Bahrain and Sheikh Abu Dhabi together.

Under these circumstances, Sheikh Jassim decided to ally with Ottomans to put an end to these transgressions. He knew that these two sheikhs would not dare to do what they did if it was not for the assistance of the British. Hence, he needed a great power to protect his country. After he had the backing of the Ottomans, he devoted his efforts to the internal political affairs. He began to call on the sheikhs of tribe for unity under the banner of Islam.

As to the Ottomans, they lost the coast of Oman, which includes Masqat and Abu Dhabi as well as Bahrain when they were busy with their wars in Europe and Crimea. Therefore, the British took that opportunity to make several treaties with local sheikhs and got their loyalty, even though their hearts were with the Ottoman Empire as Muslims.

When Midhat Pasha was appointed governor of Baghdad, he sent letters to his government in Istanbul telling that their Empire lost the coast of Oman and Bahrain to the British. He also said that they were about to take over Al-Ahsa'a, Qatif, Qatar, and their surrounding areas. After that, they would take over Kuwait. He mentioned the strategic importance of Kuwait. He suggested that they needed a strong administration in Kuwait to use it as a base to protect Al-Ahsa'a and Qatif, which fall between Bahrain and Kuwait.

Therefore, Midhat Pasha called for a meeting with the sheikhs of Kuwait in Basra. His aim was to strengthen the relation with

Kuwait so that it would not lean to the British, who always tempted other sheikhs with protection and gifts. When the Kuwaiti sheikhs came for the meeting, they had a petition of their problems and their demands. The most important items were to keep their current sheikh as a district administrator, no taxation, using the Shafi'ee sect in their court, and several others.

Midhat Pasha approved all their demands as they were within his authority. He endorsed their sheikh as the district administrator. He told them that the Ottoman government did not need their money. Its main goal was to protect the Muslims. He asked them to raise the Ottoman flag on the district administrator's palace and allow a gendarmerie force of one hundred soldiers to station in Kuwait with their salaries being paid by Kuwait.

Midhat Pasha sent a letter to Istanbul describing what was agreed upon with the sheikhs of Kuwait. The sultan issued a decree endorsing the agreement. He ordered that the Ottoman flag should be raised on the district administrator's building. Midhat Pasha ordered to resume the dates used to be sent from Basra to Kuwait, which was worth fifty thousand to sixty thousand rials. This way, Kuwait became part of the Ottoman Empire officially.

When Midhat Pasha settled the situation with Kuwait, he turned to the problem of Al-Ahsa'a and Qatif, for which he had planned the campaign as we discussed earlier. Apparently, he had in mind to include Kuwait as the base from which the troops would take off as well as using fighters and ships of Kuwait led by the Amir and his brother in the campaign.

It should be noted that if Midhat Pasha had been appointed earlier as governor of Baghdad and Basra, he might have saved the coast of Oman, including Masqat and Abu Dhabi, as well as Bahrain, from being taken over by the British. Both the newly appointed sheikh of Bahrain Isa bin Ali Al-Khalifa and Sheikh Abu Dhabi Zaid bin Khalifa officially recognized their loyalty to the British.

QATAR AS PART OF THE OTTOMAN EMPIRE

One of the accomplishments of the campaign was that Qatar became part of the Ottoman Empire voluntarily. With that, the entire Arab Gulf coast and the Arabian Peninsula became under the full control of the Ottomans. Most of these entities only nominally belonged to the Empire for centuries.

Another achievement of the campaign was the disappointment of the British. The Ottomans came out of it stronger and recognized by the Arabian tribes in the Gulf and the Arabian Peninsula. While the British had been working hard persistently to control the region, the Ottomans accomplished that in days. The Ottomans also limited the district of Abdullah Faisal to a small area of Nejd, getting the rest of the district under the rule of an Ottoman directly.

Since Mohammed Al-Thani became very old, he relinquished his sheikhdom to his son Jassim. Both father and son requested officially from Nafith Pasha, who became in charge of Al-Ahsa'a district administrator, to send them for Ottoman flags to put them on Sheikh Jassim's palace, the father's palace, the palace of Ali bin Abdullah Sheikh of the Bay Area; and the fourth flag was sent to the City of U'daid.

After that, a British ship came to Qatar to collect taxes for the sheikh of Bahrain Isa. When they met with Sheikh Jassim, he pointed to the Ottoman flag and said, "We are under this flag . . . We do not recognize anyone else as long as we are under this flag." They left Qatar empty-handed.

The Ottomans enquired from the British consulate in Baghdad and asked for an official response about the British ship that had gone to Qatar asking for taxes to be paid to Sheikh Isa. Qatar was part of Al-Ahsa'a district, which is part of the Ottoman Empire. The consul contacted the British government in India. He gave Midhat Pasha a letter stating that the British employees did not go into Qatar or ask for money. This was clearly a diplomatic answer. He did not deny the ship being in Qatar or that someone who was non-British went into Qatar and asked for the tax. The reason the British sent their ship to Qatar was to scare Sheikh Jassim. If he gave them tax money, it was an admission that Qatar belonged to Bahrain. But they failed in their plan.

The British would never give up on Qatar because it was the closest to Bahrain. The British and their appointed sheikh of Bahrain Isa took sides with Saud in his dispute with Abdullah Sheikh Nejd. They supported Saud in his attack on Al-Ahsa'a, Qatif, and the other entities on the coast of the Gulf. After he got his supplies and ammunitions from Bahrain through Qatar, Saud revenged on the sheikhs of Qatar by cutting off their drinking water and confiscating their camels and herds. He was angry with them because they had sided with the Ottomans. This happened after his defeat and flight through Qatar. Therefore, in order to stop Saud and the other sheikhs that aligned with the British from transgression on Qatar, Sheikh Jassim requested from the Ottomans to send protection. The latter sent two ships with columns from Al-Ahsa'a to Qatar and stayed for some time there. After that, peace prevailed.

Qatar Remained Independent

After the military operations of the campaign ended, the Ottomans redefined the administrative set up in the region. As we mentioned earlier, a new district was created in Al-Ahsa'a. It included also Qatif, Haffoof, Qatar, and other surrounding entities. The District of Nejd was reduced to Riyadh and its vicinities. This new reorganization came in instructions sent by Midhat Pasha. There would be an Ottoman director, a local deputy, a magistrate, and financial and administrative employees. There would be an administrative council and a judicial council.

One of the articles in the instruction excluded Qatar from having an Ottoman director, but Sheikh Jassim would be given full authority to rule Qatar. It was also exempted from appointing all other posts. It was left to Sheikh Jassim to handle that. These decisions were taken as recognition from Midhat Pasha of the role Sheikh Jassim played in the campaign and for his personal prestige.

It should be noted that before issuing the instruction, Mohammed Bey, a Turkish man, was appointed district administrator for Qatar by Nafith Pasha. He was given a salary of sixteen thousand okas (equivalent to 43,000 lbs.) of dates as an honorarium per year. When Sheikh Jassim was appointed to that post, the sultan ordered to continue the same amount or its equivalent in money. This honorarium payment was not continuously paid because of some accounting problem of recording it by the treasurer in Basra. Besides, I think that Sheikh Jassim was very rich through his pearl hunting and trading that he would not care much about it. The Ottomans should have been concerned about paying it because it symbolized dependency of Qatar on the Ottoman Empire. The question is, where did that salary go? The sultan also instructed the government that all regions should demonstrate their belonging to the Ottoman Empire.

In spite of the success in the military operations to accomplish the set goals and the zealousness of the Arabian tribe in the Gulf and Arabian Peninsula for the Ottoman leadership, the government and its policy did not follow up this success. They did not have the vision and long-term plan of the aftermath. The British, on the other hand, were able to infiltrate into the high-ranked Ottoman government to control it from within. The British also realized that what rallied most Arabian tribes behind the Ottomans and alienated them from the British was Islam. Hence, they planned to weaken their attachment to their religion. They encouraged deviation from the original Islam, spread fables, and told people, especially the educated ones, that secularism meant progressive and democratic. They worked on all types of people: the simple, illiterate people with fables, religious men with deviation from the original Islam, and the educated persons to become atheist and secular. None of these people stopped to think about why British people were still attending church, yet they encouraged Muslims to leave their religion.

* * *

SECTION 2

THE RELATION BETWEEN QATAR AND THE OTTOMANS

THE RELATION WITH SHEIKH JASSIM

It is known historically that there had been several disputes between Sheikh Jassim and the Ottoman administrators of the Basra and Nejd governorates. The main reason for such disputes was the Ottoman administrators did not like to see him with full authority over Qatar. That gave them no chance to get personal advantages from the revenues of Qatar as they used to get from other districts. They tried to smear his reputation with lies and false accusations in order to get the government to make him an obscure Ottoman employee under their control.

After about fifteen years since the campaign of Midhat Pasha, the conditions in the Nejd and other territories had deteriorated substantially. It required administrative reform and protection. Qatar remained under Sheikh Jassim's rule. According to the earlier decision, the Ottoman government could not replace him without his consent.

What looked like a sudden awakening of the Ottoman government, a new plan was designed by the new governor of Nejd A'akif Pasha. The plan came late, about fifty years. He received some instructions from Istanbul and his study of the entire region; he came up with a reform program for Nejd and all the Gulf coastal entities. He sent it to Istanbul on June 9, 1889, for approval. It contained six articles. We shall cite some of it in the following:

ARTICLE 1

Improve the relations between the sheikhs of tribes and their constituents and prevent the oppression of some sheikhs. Strengthen the bonds and ties between people and the Ottoman Empire. Most people are religiously adherent. That is why they accepted any judgments based on Islamic jurisprudence. But they had difficulty in yielding to secular laws and legislations because of their bedouin nature. They had been accustomed to following their sheikh, whom they selected and gave their allegiance. Therefore, to spend 120,000 rials every year did not accomplish anything. They had to understand that there is another level of authority above that of their sheikh, but it does not belittle or override the authority of their sheikh. We suggest abolishing the justice department temporarily. Secular cases should be referred to the administrative council. But the religious cases (marriage, divorce, etc.) will go to deputy and his staff, who will be appointed in Qatif. Any political problem will be referred to the command of the army.

ARTICLE 2

Since Sheikh Bahrain followed the British, we should establish protective force from the Ottoman Empire. We should attract their sheikh toward us and gradually change him. We should avoid irritation of the British or its objection. It should be noted that changing the sheikh of Bahrain is not advisable. The people of Bahrain are Muslims. Hence, when there is judicial case, they will not follow but the Islamic jurisprudence. They appointed an Islamic magistrate to decide their disputes. Therefore, they are more likely to lean toward the amir of the believers the Caliph. On the other hand, Nassir Al-Mubarak, who was appointed by the Ottoman government and resides in Al-Ahsa'a. After they were defeated by the British, they go to Bahrain every five to ten days to have a parade and anchor their ship near Bahrain to make a show in front of the Bahrainis. The Ottoman government does not make such a parade to show its control of the region.

At this time, it is difficult to induce Bahrain to the Ottoman side. All we see in the region are British ships. There is no Ottoman ship in the area. This reflects badly on people. Therefore, we should change their feeling that the Ottomans do exist and its government has great power. It has ships with high efficiency and excellent skill in maneuvering and bombing. This will let us win people's hearts and respect. This requires the use of two ships to carry the mail and merchandise between Basra and ports of Qatif, Bahrain, Qatar, and Oman. Another two ships go through the Red Sea to the ports of Yanbu and Jeddah, then to Bombay, Karachi, Masqat, Bender Abbas, Lenja, and Boshihr to arrive at Basra. These ships should move continuously.

These ships should have tourist and trade agencies. When any ship arrives at the port, there should be an Ottoman flag on a pole to welcome the ship. Besides, the flag should be raised every Friday, holidays, and the anniversary of the sultan's Inauguration Day. The government should also rent a storage house in each of the aforementioned ports or harbors. The ships that exist in Basra are not good enough to show the power of the Ottoman Empire. They should be replaced with five new warships. It is necessary to establish storage for coal so that the Ottoman ships will visit Bahrain to get their coal supplies.

The warship in Basra used to go to the coasts of the Gulf and back to Basra. This ship used to stay in any port until the other ships came. For three months, no ship has crossed to the coasts of Nejd. Hence, the matter was presented to the governor, but nothing happened. Things had got back to its old situation of slackness. Until the arrival of the four mail ships that run between the Red Sea to Basra—there had to be at least one warship every month to go between Basra and Nejd coasts. This is necessary to be close to any event that may happen and chase after the pirates. This will have positive effects on the people of the region and reflect on the power of the Ottoman Empire and erase the rumors about the weakness of the Ottomans. Such efforts would lead to the control of the Ottoman government in the territories under its rule and encourage Bahrain and other entities that became under the British control to go back to the Ottomans.

Article 3

There are several affairs requiring discussion to take decisions about them. Among them is to appoint Sheikh Nassir Al-Mubarak, who resides now in Al-Ahsa'a, the amir of Bahrain instead of the current amir. Another issue is to increase the maritime and land forces. A third one is to improve on the administration of Riyadh and Oman and upgrade them to become governorates and to extend telegram lines to Al-Ahsa'a.

To appoint Sheikh Nassir Al-Mubarak amir of Bahrain will cause bloodshed and the protest of the British. Hence, it should postpone the idea for now. But if the Ottoman government showed its power and presence in the region by sending the four warships to roam around in the Gulf, people will rally around the Ottoman Empire for their adherence to Islam. This way it comes from within Bahrain.

To appoint a governor for each of Riyadh and Oman is very necessary. Riyadh falls about seven days from the governorate center Haffoof. This distance is acceptable. Besides, Haffoof does not have drinking water. But the revenues from Riyadh are more than that of Haffoof. Hence, in order to manage the administration of this district, they required seven hundred cavalrymen and two columns for each of Riyadh and Haffoof. There should be camps to house them. In order to rule Oman, it was required to appoint a governor, use ships to run the mail, bring in five hundred camels, and two battalions of cavalrymen and extend telegraph lines to the area. A'aqeer is considered the most important harbor on the coast.

We find that the sultan and the prime minister are determined to implement this idea. The sultan ordered one thousand liras in addition to all the revenues from the region to extend the telegraph lines and whatever was necessary for the plan. He invited the dignitaries and merchants to the government palace. He incited them in a nice way, encouraging, and explained the benefit for the project of telegraph network. This project was extended to all the Arabian Peninsula, Ethiopia, the Red Sea, and the Arab Gulf. A map was constructed of the network and sent to Istanbul for final approval. The entire region of the Arab Gulf—the Arabian Peninsula, the Red Sea, and the Arabian Sea—will benefit from the project and will be grateful to the Ottoman Empire. It is important to provide the necessary security for the network.

ARTICLE 4

As for the dismissal of the current sheikh of Bahrain and appointment of another instead, Article 4 should be studied carefully and the necessary action taken to implement it.

ARTICLE 5

SUGGESTIONS ABOUT QATAR

There should be a qualified director appointed for Zibara, which is in the north of Qatar. He will be given one thousand piasters and provided with forty to fifty cavalrymen under his leadership. Another director of high qualifications will be appointed in U'daid at the southern area of Qatar with 750 Piasters and send several officers to the area.

Since the port of Qatar is very large, and because of so many Western and foreign ships anchor there, a chief of port will be appointed who is fluent in Arabic and familiar with inspection of passengers other port affairs. A deputy district administrator will be appointed for Sheikh Jassim with a salary of two thousand Piasters. He should be well versed in the Arabic language and knowledgeable in politics to assist in securing stability in the entity. Most of the people of Qatar are poor. They get their living from fishing, and the others work for wages in the pearl hunting. Therefore, not many of them can work as members of council or clerks unless they are paid salaries. Some of the Qataris could be employed as clerks administrating assistance, and letter writers were to be paid between 250–500 piasters. The Ottoman government should develop Qatar, especially Zibara and U'daid.

As it is applied in the Qatif and A'aqeer harbors, custom duties will be collected in the port of Qatar. Then gradually, port tax will be levied from ship owners. It is expected to get 2,500 liras per annum. In that way, we shall close the door in the face of the foreigners, affairs will be better, security will prevail, and that will leave great impression on the people of the Arabian Peninsula. If the situation of the treasury is studied carefully, economizing in the expenditures to carry out the plan, great benefits for the people will occur, businesses will flourish, and the rights of the Empire will be protected in these areas.

As for the entities that will be taken over by the Ottomans, security and peace of mind will be guaranteed. Employing some qualified personnel and sending soldiers and officers to these areas gets people to support the government, strengthen the security system, and eliminate gangs and bandits to relieve people from their transgression. At the same time, spread justice in the appropriate ways; distribute gifts and charities to the needy. Besides, these regions will be treated differently than those other possessions of the Empire. Since gangs and bandits are usually five- to six-day distances from the cities, the Ottoman government provides five hundred camels and two battalions of cavalrymen to chase those outlaw bedouins.

The Fatal Mistake in the A'akif Reform Plan

The A'akif Pasha reform program can be considered the beginning of subsidence of the Ottomans' rule. Its timing was not appropriate, it lacked sufficient information about the society, and it did not take into consideration Sheikh Jassim's reaction. Hence, it created a boundary of mistrust between Sheikh Jassim and the Ottomans. It appeared that behind the attempt of the Ottomans to hold with strong grip on Qatar and establish custom duty office was the complaint submitted by Persian merchants to the district administrator of Al-Ahsa'a that Sheikh Jassim had overburdened them with taxes. Therefore, without due investigation whether this was a true or false accusation to smear Sheikh Jassim's reputation with the Ottomans, the latter took inappropriate actions.

It was quite usual for the Ottomans, especially the governors and their subordinates, to rush into decisions without deep study or to ask for advice. They were mostly arrogant and resorted to showing their muscles in solving the problems. Most of the Ottoman employees did not have the Islamic manners of humbleness to consider other people as their brothers. However, there were some governors and lower-ranked employees who were adherent to Islam and followed the manners in accordance with the teaching of the Prophet (peace be upon him).

It was quite unfortunate for someone who wanted to introduce changes in the administration of the area; he did not understand the Arabic society, especially the tribal ties and traditions. He even did not have a good idea about the history and geography of the region of which he wanted to improve its setup. A'akif Pasha, the governor of Nejd, had a good reform program, but his bad manners (arrogance and dominating personality) led him to commit mistakes that ruined his program. Most Ottoman governors and their subordinates were thinking of the Arabs and their sheikhs as cookie cutters; that is, once they know one, all others are the same.

A'akif Pasha did not know that Qatar and its sheikh Jassim were different than other areas or sheikhs he knew. Sheikh Jassim was so rich that A'akif could not induce him with money to submit to his orders. He did not submit to the threat of the British. Hence, A'akif was wrong in thinking that with his program of many points, including making Qatar under the Ottoman government administratively and financially by hiring Ottoman personnel in different posts, it could isolate Sheikh Jassim and shrink his domain of ruling. A'akif did not bother himself to consult Sheikh Jassim about his program, especially what concerned Qatar. The directors for Zibara and U'daid could not even report to their post. The chief of port was redirected for Qatif to do something else.

A'akif Pasha overlooked the fact that Qatar was Sheikh Jassim. For example, the German explorer Herman Burkhart had to ask Sheikh Jassim about going around Qatar and taking photos, which he did not have to do elsewhere. After the government reviewed the program of A'akif Pasha, it was decided to postpone the Bahrain issue and to concentrate on the part that concerned Qatar, as if the program was designed for Qatar. But the program included abolishing the judicial system, which was earmarked in the budget 120,000 piasters, to support it and apply it. Appoint an efficient and knowledgeable magistrate for each of Haffoof and Qatif. Local people would not accept any person for their cases except magistrate of their sect. They had never taken their cases to the court appointed by the Ottomans; that was different.

A'akif Pasha assumed that his program should be approved by the government in Istanbul. Therefore, he began to take steps in executing it. He asked for five hundred camels to use in his military operations against the bedouins, whose transgressions increased, and he had to stop them immediately. He sent his request to the Basra governorate. Since they were delayed in their response, he sent his request to the Interior Ministry, stating,

> The bedwin tribes keep killing people and stealing their belongings. They even once stopped the mail carrier took the mail and the camels and killed the mailman. If they were not chased with camels and troops, they will not only continue, but others will be encouraged to follow suit. Camels are the only means of going after those bandits. We desperately need these camels as soon as possible to restore peace and security in the region.

> We may remind your Excellency of the attack carried out by Sheikh Zaid of Abu Dhabi on Qatar. They killed people and confiscated their movable properties and burn down houses. If I had the 500 camels and the soldiers, I would have prevented this massacre. We can bring those transgressors to the right path. We will be able to collect zakat. Since this issue is vitally important, I wrote you directly.

It is interesting to note that A'akif Pasha, who is a lieutenant general in the army, brought the attack of Sheikh Zaid on southern Qatar as an example. He said that he would have prevented the massacre. He was in Nejd, which on camels is ten to twelve days away from the area attacked by Sheikh Zaid. The distance between Abu Dhabi and southern Qatar is two to three days by camels. This means that for A'akif to know about the incident, Sheikh Zaid would have been back in his hometown drinking coffee. This indicates how naive these Ottoman generals and district administrators are.

Although the program was ambitious, only a few points were executed. The Ottoman Empire had shrunken quite a lot, especially when nominal related regions were included. This plan was supposed to be the last savior of the Empire if was sincerely designed and executed. In the beginning of the twentieth century, there were changes in the political situation in Bahrain and Oman. The Ottoman government showed some languish in carrying out these suggestions of A'akif program and had no enthusiasm to do anything as the cancer had already spread in the body of the Empire.

Two years had passed since the approval of the government in Istanbul of the program of A'akif Pasha. The government of Istanbul inquired of the Basra governor how much of the program had been executed. The governor answered that nothing of the program had been executed concerning Qatar because Sheikh Jassim had not approved any of the changes in his territory. Sheikh Jassim had a strong personality, and he was in full control of Qatar and its tribes. As to the issue of telegraph lines and the mail ships, there had been no movement of starting these projects. Mohammed Hidayat, governor of Basra, January 29, 1892.

* * *

CHAPTER 7

QATAR INCIDENT OR WEJBA BATTLE

PREFACE

Before we go into the details of the decisive incident in the modern history of Qatar, we should go back a little to look into the knowledge of the Ottoman administration and how they looked to the delicate tribal society in the region. Besides, there were inherited problems of the Ottoman administration. There were always contradictions between the demands of the sultan and the Cabinet on one hand, and the bad manners and behavior of most governors and their subordinates who worked in the Gulf and the Arabian Peninsula.

Most of these administrators had a low level of general knowledge and did not know Arabic; they did not have the ability to deal with special characteristics of the region and had no knowledge of the Arab traditions and habits. These administrators were causing great headaches to the decision center and the caliph. If we knew that the Muslim caliph was Sultan Abdul Hameed,[21] the decision about such problems and undesirable events must take into consideration and look into the consequences of how the subjects of the caliph would look to the caliph.

The Muslim Caliph: Sultan Abdul Hameed the Second

Sultan Abdul Hameed was a good Muslim. He liked the Arabs and respected their sheikhs, especially Sheikh Jassim, to whom he gave him special treatment. In spite of the conspiracies of some Ottoman governors or district administrators, the sultan did not pay attention to them. The sultan was trying very hard to keep his nation together and encourage the harmony among the people and with their administrators. He used great effort to get Muslims to adhere to their religion to achieve unity and harmony. However, the situation in the Arabian Peninsula and its adjunct regions remained bad because the Ottoman administrators were poor, inefficient, and corrupt. If we look at Nejd, the gangs and bandits increased, becoming very dangerous. It affected people's lives as trade ceased to exist. At the same time, Ottoman employees were busy looking for their own interests by overtaxing people to be rich before they went back to their country.

The only way the government in Istanbul could, perhaps, look after complaints of the people was to change the governor or the administrator about whom there were complaints. Such a policy led to make the bad situation worse. Since the new governor or administrator knew that he was replacing a corrupt one, he tried to collect as much money as possible before Istanbul would find out about him. This situation left a bad impression on people of the area, especially Nejd. It led merchants from Nejd to write a petition signed by thirty-six merchants sent to the office of the Cabinet in Istanbul on May 22, 1892. It contained the following:

> Although, we are under the umbrella of safety and security of the Sultan, the bandits high jacked a caravan 3 years ago. It was going toward Al-Ahsa'a from A'aqeer. They confiscated all the merchandize on it, which was huge amount. They killed people and let women and children die in the desert. The criminals were not punished in any way. That is why we hired guards from all tribes and told the local Government to secure the safety of our caravans. We paid the guards salaries from us. Even though we tried this method which is the best we can do, the situation remained the same.

> Since these criminals were not disciplined, they took such crimes as their way of living by confiscating merchandize and kidnapping children and women until they were paid ransoms. Besides, the local Government made no effort to chase the criminals to return the merchandize to their rightful owners, more bandits joined the other gangs. The salaries that the Government has been paying the tribes spoiled them. Therefore, the Government lost its dignity and respect. If the Government continues to pay the tribes salaries

and provide them with what they asked for, the situation will be worse than it is now.

Those who dare to do these crimes in Nejd because it is sparsely populated but very poor at the same time, they find these activities easy to do and greatly rewarded, especially if they knew that the Government would not be after them. In May 1892, some bandits raided on a caravan belong to very rich merchants and dignitaries who were going to India, Bahrain and Basra. They had with them large amounts of silver coins, rupees and liras as well as large quantities of precious merchandise valued at 20,000 Liras. The criminals stole everything including the animals and killed Abdul Aziz bin Fahd who is renowned merchant. These merchants and dignitaries thought that they are protected by the Government of the Sultan.

We know the leaders of these criminals. They are Rashid bin Mana', Faraj bin Hlaiman and his brother Daham. They get help from some tribes in the outskirts of Al-Ahsa'a and Oman. Sheikh Abu Dhabi supply them with men. This brings shame to the Ottoman Empire. It is well known to the Prime Minister, that the taxes levied from people are supposed to be used for their protection. It is also known that laws and regulations of the Ottoman Government are not just words, but to be applied. This situation is the result of lack of sincerity of the employees.

The District of Nejd is not less politically than any other district. We are your followers and obedient to the Ottoman Government. We pay our dues and the cost of public services and more. This should not be accepted by the high authority to have such shortcomings to happen. Perhaps, some of these dues did not reach the Treasury and were not recovered even after our complaints. Government employees only think of how they could get rich from the poor who cannot refuse paying even if the taxes or duties are not lawful. They try to send more money to the Treasury in Istanbul to get rewarded and promoted. They pretend to use justice in their behavior.

Government stability depends on the action of its army in protecting people and prevent the use of arms by people that under its control. When tribes are using arms against innocent merchants, the local administrators should follow the Central Government's instructions in that respect. At least soldiers should be dispatched immediately to the place of any robbery to capture the criminals.

When this petition will reach high authority, the local employees will deny wrong doing and pretend that everything here is alright. They will blame the problems on others. The disasters that took place and the situation in Nejd as presented to you are true. If nothing happens to make us secure, we have to leave Nejd to somewhere else. We cannot stay and endanger our families, ourselves and our properties any longer. The soldiers of the Sultan should go after these criminals and punish them. But to give them money and gifts will not deter them.

These criminals reside in place near our residence. Therefore, they monitor our movements. This led to abandon the roads that pass through them, which mean the region became under blockade. In spite of submission a petition to the Government to retrieve our stolen property, but nothing happened. This is why we resorted to the highest authority for solution. If you do not take immediate action to protect us, we have to move to another more secure place.

We are all under the Mercy of Allah and we all shall return to Him. We are awaiting your order and decision from your Excellency.

The Governor of Basra, Hafidh Pasha, took the opportunity of the aforementioned petition sent by Nejd merchants as a good excuse and strong argument to dispatch a military campaign toward Al-Ahsa'a, then Qatar. He claimed that Sheikh Jassim and his domination in the region were behind the problems of Nejd. Of course, the governor's hatred of Sheikh Jassim and his influence over Qatar and the surrounding regions led the governor to get rid of him.

The Nejd merchants were complaining about the repeated robbery operations and not one incident. In fact, they pointed out about the few criminals and named them in their petition that were in the Nejd area. The merchants indicated that the problem was the bad behavior of the employees in the Nejd District. Hafidh Pasha used those corrupt employees in Nejd to turn the case against Sheikh Jassim. After his several false accusations against Sheikh Jassim, with which the governor attempted to smear his reputation with the Istanbul government, this was a good chance to get rid of him militarily. There are several indications that the British had their hands involved in the rumors about Sheikh Jassim because he remained firm against the British attempts to penetrate into Qatar to become part of the coast from Oman to Basra. In fact, the British resident in Boshihr mentioned that clearly.

The Qatar Incident as Was Told by the Basra Governor

The following is the letter of the governor of Basra to the prime minister explaining what happened in what is known as the Qatar incident or the Wejba battle.

> To his Excellency the Prime Minister; In order to lift the disobedience and remove the criminal acts from Nejd, we moved to Al-Ahsa'a, the central Government of Nejd and its surroundings with the sniper battalion #11 which has about 200 men. As a result of our action, security has prevailed in these areas. However, since the instigator for the criminal acts in Nejd has been for two months Sheikh Jassim, the District Administrator. He has been in that post for 25 years. He was taking the revenues of about a million for himself. He refused to let in the Ottoman employees who were sent 2 years ago. He, Sheikh Jassim, took over Haffoof from Nejd to be with Qatar 2 years ago. Therefore, we thought that to solve the problem and maintain security in the entire region, we went with the same battalion to Qatar 40 days ago. In spite of the taking over the castle that he built for his son Khalifa and the cannons that were there, he disappeared with 400 of his men from the tribes of Manaseer, Beni Hager and other tribes before the arrival of your servant in a month. We tried to persuade him to disperse his men, but he did not listen at all. Instead he insisted to delay the formation of the judicial system by encouraging people to that effect.

When we learned that he intended to attack Doha, he is holding the road between Qatar and Al-Ahsa'a and he stopped the mailman to take the papers and burned them, we had to do something to stop him. We arrested his brother Ahmad and 10 others of his men. We found out through our spies that these men were trying to arrange the attack. After we took over his fortress which is about 2 hours from the District headquarter and recorded the number of cannons, then we consulted with the military officers with us, we included 30 soldiers to our battalion. We also brought in sufficient marines and ship cannons in addition to 140 cavalry. We took off from the City the 12th of February. After we arrived near a small castle situated near the fortress, some firing on our front troops followed by an attack on them. Our troops resisted the rebels and caused them great losses. Then most of the battalion went in the fortress without any fight. It became impossible to get them out. We noticed that most of the soldiers and officers do not follow the directives of the battalion commander. We found out that the best solution was to retreat systematically to avoid the siege around the fortress. Although, we went 10 minutes without incident, about 5 Calvary from among about 70 horsemen attacked us. They were joined by the other Calvary men. Our losses were 150 soldiers and 8 officers between dead or injured. Besides, the rebellions got cannon.

Your servant went to the ship Mirreekh immediately to direct the war; internal or external as doomed necessary as well as defend the City from the sea and stand against any rebellions from abroad. The Colonel Hussein Rami gave me a memorandum telling me that the soldiers inside the fortress are not enough to fight. We made contact with the officers and soldiers who are in the fortress and sent Colonel Rami to the fortress, but he returned to the ship injured in his shoulder. We noticed from the ship that there are some men firing at the soldiers who were trying to leave the fortress. We started to fire from the cannon of the ship on those rebels. What remained in the fortress were about 100 soldiers and few officers and one physician. After the last fight, we sent Colonel Youssef to the fortress again.

The purpose of Sheikh Jassim's move was to leave the District for him as independent. Then he aimed to use the bedwins to take over Al-Ahsa'a and its surrounding entities. It seems, after all what happened, that Sheikh Jassim started to look for more territories. On the other hand, after we freed his brother, according to our investigation, he was planning to continue his siege of the fortress and take over Al-Ahsa'a. Therefore, I beg you with all my feeling of the importance to send 4–5 battalions and 2–3 cannons under the leadership of Lieutenant General Kadhim Pasha of the sixth army as soon as possible in a ship. (the governor of Basra, Hafidh, March 14, 1893)

These are the details of the Wejba Battle or what is called the Qatar Incident in the *Ottoman Archive* as reported by Hafidh Pasha, according to his claim of its reason and how it happened. He sent his report to Basra. But it did not reach Istanbul until March 27. The Cabinet sent the request for reinforcements to the sultan for approval the same day.

<<Photo #4>>
Wejba Castle as pictured in the 1950s

SULTAN ABDUL HAMEED
ORDERED INVESTIGATION

Sultan Abdul Hameed ordered that an immediate detailed investigation of the problem be reported to him personally. The order was sent as a telegram to Mr. Sa'eed, the chief of the dignitaries of Basra. The telegram was as follows:

> In order to conduct investigation of the reasons for the fights in the District of Qatar in details and inform those who were involved in this issue and the consequences of such irresponsible acts, we want you to go to Qatar with two men to investigate the matter thoroughly. The details of your mission shall be sent to the Prime Minister. To carry out this task properly is vitally important because it received great concern by the Caliph the Sultan.

> According to what stated above, we ask you to give the matter your extreme effort and full attention to achieve your task in the best way and that is what expected of you. This order is in accordance with the desire of the Caliph who was informed of this telegram.

THE WEJBA BATTLE AS WAS
TOLD BY SHEIKH JASSIM

Sheikh Jassim rushed to send a letter with mail ship to Sa'eed Effendi, the chief of the dignitaries in Basra. He expected that the

ship must be carrying big accusations against him. The letter reached
Mr. Sa'eed on March 31, 1893. He immediately gave a copy of it to
be sent in a telegram to the sultan. He said the following in his letter:

> Peace is upon you and Allah Mercy. I first would
> like to ask about how you are doing. You know,
> your Honorable Esquire that the Governor of
> Basra Hafidh Pasha came to us in Qatar with
> land troops and warships from the sea. When we
> realized that there were no dignitaries like your-
> self or any of the renowned Arabs to whom we
> consider as model, we were apprehensive and
> stayed away from him leaving the country for
> him. We warned the tribes from confronting him
> or doing anything against him. When he arrived
> at Al-Dira, he informed me that he wanted to
> see me. I apologized telling him that I do not
> feel safe with you. He gave me covenant with
> Allah and the safety of the Sultan that nothing
> will happen to me. I sent my brother Ahmad to
> him to tell him that Sheikh Jassim is an old man
> and could not come. He is telling you that we
> are all under the custody of Allah first then the
> Sultan. I also told him that I shall do whatever it
> is required of me.
>
> However, he did not listen to my apology, but he
> broke his promise and imprisoned my brother.
> Although, he gave the safety to all the people
> of A-Dira by an announcer, but he betrayed his
> promise and arrested the dignitaries of the City
> and put them in prison.
>
> When I saw him acting like that, my fears
> increased so as my alienation of him. I wrote
> him asking for the release of my brother and the

other dignitaries whom he arrested as a mercy of the Sultan. If he wanted anything, I shall give him from my own money, but he did not listen. Hafidh pasha persisted in his aggression and severity with us. He did not follow the laws and regulation of the Ottoman Government, unlike the manners of Nafith Pasha who came to Qatar before. Therefore, when I saw that there is no use to straighten him up, I decided to leave Qatar reliant on Allah and to send my grievance to Government in Istanbul. I left him in Qatar to do whatever he wished. I ordered the tribes to disperse as they see fit.

When he heard that I was about to leave Qatar and I asked the tribes to disperse, ordered the troops to attack us on the 6th of Ramadan. We heard the sound of bombing and people were screaming. Hafidh Pasha attacked the tribes between my residence and Al-Dira. When the two sides clashed, he fled on his horse to the ship. He left his soldiers fighting for themselves with the tribes. Then the killings and lootings started. The following day, when I heard that soldiers being killed, I came to stop the killing. But the Governor remained on the ship. I asked him to release my brother and the other prisoners and his soldiers will be safe, he did not listen or cared about the soldiers. Perhaps, because he was astonished and fearful of what happened.

I tried my best and announce to the soldiers that anyone wanted to go to the ship can go, or if they wanted to go to Al-Ahsa'a, I shall send a force to protect them. Finally if anyone would like to stay in Qatar, he is welcome. I assume that

Hafidh Pasha sent with a small ship to Basra to present the situation untruly. Your Honorable knows about us and that we offer good service to the Empire. We have never been except to what pleases the Sultan. However, what happened this time was the bad conduct of Hafidh Pasha.

Meeting of the Cabinet

The information that came out from the two rivals concerning the reasons for the Qatar incident, how it happened, and whether it was for self-defense were discussed in a meeting in Istanbul at the highest level. It came in the minutes of the meeting, which was held on April 2, 1893, to discharge Hafidh Pasha from his job according to the decision that came from the sultan, before the investigating committee finished its fact-finding.

The minutes include the report sent by Hafidh Pasha in which he told his view of the reason he attacked Qatar, what happened during the fight, and the accomplishments. While he blamed everything on Sheikh Jassim, he showed himself as a hero caring for his soldiers. The minutes then turned to the version of Sheikh Jassim of the reason, what happened, and the end result. How Hafidh Pasha left his soldiers in a dangerous situation to save himself by going to the ship and hide there. Sheikh Jassim indicated his loyalty to the sultan and that he himself volunteered to merge Qatar with the Ottoman Empire without a fight.

It is imperative that there is a wide gap between the two versions, which makes it very hard for reconciliation to come up with the true version. For the Supreme Council, Hafidh Pasha was the governor of Basra, whose view had to be taken with consideration. Sheikh Jassim, on the other hand, was well respected by the sultan. However, it seems that the member of that Council read between the lines and used their unbiased judgment to come up with their recommendation as stated above. They wanted to be sure of what actually happened and why. They formed a fact-finding committee of Rassim Bieg, the commander of the 41 Brigade; Sa'eed Afandi, chief of the honorable dignitaries of Basra; and the amir of Kuwait, Mohammed Al-Sabah, or his brother Mubarak.

Incidentally, in the minutes, we gave a summary of above. There was mention of "your slave" so-and-so many times, referring to the governor, commander, even the prime minister as slaves of the sultan. In addition to be forbidden in Islam, as everybody including prophets being slaves of Allah. If someone refers to himself as a servant of another person, regardless of the latter position, it is considered an association partnership with Allah, which is forbidden. It is also tasteless and unacceptable socially.

The Qatar Incident According to the Fact-Finding Committee

Sa'eed Afandi went to Qatar with the rest of the fact-finding committee (FFC). Their primary goal was reconciliation between the two factions by reducing the tension. It also wanted to advise Sheikh Jassim to continue his allegiance to the Ottoman Empire and carry out his duties as Ottoman district administrator of Qatar. The FFC took the warship *Mejdersan* on June 30, 1893.

The FFC arrived after five days in the Port of Qatar early in the morning. They met Sheikh Ahmad, Sheik Jassim's brother, then later met with Sheikh Jassim who came down from his Fortress Wejba to the city. The FFC visited the fortress and listened to Sheikh Jassim describe the incident. After the hearing, they wrote a report on September 10, 1893. We give some of it:

> Sheikh Jassim claimed that nothing came out of him against the pleasure of the Sultan in the 25 years. He said that he sent several plea letters to Hafidh Pasha. He sent his sons, brother and men offering to submit to the orders of the Government, but the person he is referring to did not accept. Therefore, in accordance to his orders, the tribes around him were dispersed. He

decided to obey, but the Ottoman forces started
the attack one day Wejba Fortress. He tried to
stay away and disappear, but his family was with
him and the tribesmen while trying to disperse,
they heard the sound of fired bullets from the
soldiers. The tribesmen came together and began
to resist the soldiers. I did not approve that or
even knew about it. We (FFC) did not believe
him. We found out that Sheikh Jassim's son
Thani injured in his left arm during the battle.
We also saw how Sheikh Jassim was concerned
with Sheikh Sultan, who led the rebels when
they disarmed the Ottoman soldiers and killed
them. He also was gracious with Sief Al-Hajiri
and other chiefs of tribes who participated in the
battle. Our investigations led us to the fact that
Sheikh Jassim himself was on his horse in the battle wearing white head cover killing some of the
officers.

We (FFC) showed Sheikh Jassim the evidences
we got in a nice way. We then explained to him
that the Sultan knew the truth, but his kindness
to his fellow Muslims, like the father to his son
enough forces to discipline the tribesmen and
punish them.

Accordingly, it is your loyalty to the Caliph and
his mercy, that the people of Qatar should return
and meet with the soldiers showing them nice
treatment and spread peace and security in Qatar.
They all should make supplications 5 times a day
(that is in each prayer). You have to facilitate the
mission of Sa'eed Afandi who was ordered to take
care of the weapons and taxes.

After we finish talking to Sheikh Jassim, he said in defense of his position that the British Consul at Boshihr came to him after the Wejba battle and offered him the protection of the British, but he refused. He added that he request to be relieved from his post as District Administrator because of his old age. After he mentioned that, we asked him to explain the true reasons for his resignation. We also wanted to know the discrepancy in his claims and his intention about Bahrain in details. The FCC submitted all its findings, the presentation of Sheikh Jassim, the report of Hafidh Pasha and the resignation of Sheikh Jassim.

The investigation that was undertaken by Ahmed Mudhafar and Ismael, who were with FFC, gave details and accurate findings about what happened in the battle of Wejba. The following is a summary of what they wrote:

It seems that Hafidh Pasha took two-hundred-plus snipers and went last year to Nejd to stop the troublemakers. He was successful in his mission. But he was told that the stimulator of these robberies was Sheikh Jassim. Besides, the British complained to the Ottoman Empire against Sheikh Jassim, stating that he was behind all the disturbances and insecurity in the coasts of the Gulf. Hafidh Pasha told the FFC that Sheikh Jassim did not pay the taxes he collected to the Ottomans.

Hafidh Pasha used the same sniper battalion and added to it more soldiers to invade Qatar. When he found out that Sheikh Jassim had withdrawn with tribesmen to the desert, he advised Sheikh Jassim to surrender and show his obedience to the empire. he refused to meet Hafidh Pasha. Instead, Sheikh Jassim offered ten thousand liras as a gift and paid for all the expenses of the troops. Hafidh Pasha insisted that Sheikh Jassim must disperse the tribesmen with him and come to meet him.

Sheikh Jassim knew that Hafidh Pasha wanted to get rid of him. The latter claimed that Sheikh Jassim gathered about one thousand men and attacked Mubarak, the brother of Sheikh Kuwait, who was coming to assist Hafidh Pasha in Qatar. Hafidh Pasha heard that Sheikh Jassim was going to attack his soldiers; he sent 150 snipers with axes to scout the Wejba Fortress and destroy it. But the tribesmen attacked the soldiers. The latter defended themselves in a brave way. The tribesmen were far more in number that the soldiers. Hence, the soldiers tried to withdraw to the fortress, but they lost ninety-seven and fifty were injured.

Hafidh Pasha was helped to escape to the ship. The officers were trying to save the soldiers who were trapped in the fortress with the tribesmen surrounding them. While the soldiers were leaving the fortress at night, there were some tribesmen shooting at them. Then it was ordered to shoot twenty bombs from SS *Mirreekh* and ten from SS *Mejdersan*. Some of the soldiers were housed in the ships. There were some soldiers that remained in the fortress. They were prevented from leaving by the tribesmen unless Hafidh Pasha released the Qatar dignitaries; he held them imprisoned.

On the twelfth of April, the British consul in Boshihr came to the strait of Qatar on a ship. He claimed to seek reconciliation between Hafidh Pasha and Sheikh Jassim. The latter refused on the ground that he did not want any interference of the British. His ship was denied anchorage in the Port of Qatar. A British warship picked up the consul to take him to Wekra, three hours from Qatar, on the twenty-first of April, to meet Sheikh Jassim, who declined his intercession.

The Wejba Battle According to Al-Thani Heritage

Sheikh Mohammed bin Ahmad Al-Thani, Sheikh Jassim's nephew, wrote about the Qatar incident or the Wejba Battle. He called it the Turkish War. He thought that it was a game or conspiracy by the British to create hostility between Qatar and the Ottoman

Empire. The British sent a complaint to the Ottoman government accusing Sheikh Jassim of being the only reason for the unlawful activities in the coasts of the Gulf. The following is the exact script of Sheikh Mohammed:

THE TURKISH WAR

The Turkish War happened because of the complaint submitted by the British to the Ottoman Government saying in it that Jassim became refuge to anyone who wanted to do unlawful activities in the Gulf. Besides, the people of Al-Ahsa'a sent complaints to the Ottoman Government claimed that everything stolen from A'deed and Al-Ahsa'a were being sold in Qatar. Hence, Mohammed Hafidh Pasha took off from Basra to capture Jassim. Since Jassim had had friends in Basra, they told him about the news. But the Pasha ordered Mohammed bin Sabah (the Amir of Kuwait) to prepare an army to go to Qatar. He sent his brother Mubarak with an army from Kuwait and other tribes. The Pasha arrived Al-Ahsa'a to be joined by 400 from mercenaries of A'akeel and Muntifiq tribes. Then Abdul Rahman bin Faisal and Abdullah bin Sa'adoun came from Nejd with 3 battalions and 250 cavalrymen.

On the first day of Ramadan, the Pasha sent for Jassim to come for reconciliation. But Jassim was aware of the Pasha's intention. He sent his brother Ahmad on his behalf and left Doha to stay in Wejba. When Ahmad arrived, the Pasha refused to see him and insisted on Jassim to come personally. Ahmad kept coming to see the Pasha until the last time when he gave the Pasha Jassim's resignation from the Turkish post of Qatar and that Jassim delegated his authority to Ahmad. The Pasha was very angry and told Ahmad did the people of Doha approved you? Why Jassim evading to see me? The Pasha ordered Ahmad to return and bring the dignitaries of Doha to hear from them that they approved you as District Administrator. Ahmad returned to Doha and took 12 of the chiefs of all tribes or families plus a man who knew Turkish language. After the Governor made sure that they accepted Ahmad as their Sheikh, he told them you did not pay your taxes in the last 15 years. They told him that was not true. They added that they did not have palm tree farms or real estate, but they work in the diving for pearls, which is a 6 month season. If you demand from us money, we would pay 50,000 French Rials and the country is in your hands.

The Governor ordered the guards to take the arms from Ahmad and his companions. They all surrendered their weapons, except Mohammed bin Al-Hajji refused to give up his weapon. He told Ahmad that after taking our weapons, nothing left but killing us. He added; listen to me and let us go back. Ahmad swore at him. But bin Al-Hajji told Ahmad that I see what you do not see and left on his horse to the Wejba. When he arrived Wejba, Jassim asked him what happened to the group? He told him the story and added that I think they were arrested. After 2 hours, the news came that the group was imprisoned; the Turks took over Jassim's house and prevented the residents of Doha from leaving it.

The Governor ordered Mubarak bin Sabah to attack Jassim and his followers. Jassim gathered people of Qatar who were with him to tell them that the Governor was after me personally and I am rich so I can ransom myself. He ordered them to disperse so no harm would come to them . Most of the tribes returned to their residences. They asked Isa bin Ali, Sheikh Bahrain, to go there, he welcomed them. However, Jassim asked Sheikh Isa to accept him but he refused. He asked Sheikh Zaid to go to Oman, he too refused. He sent Shaheen Al-Timimi to Sheikh Mubarak, but it was too late for the cannons started to fire and the residents of Doha fled. Several tribes sneaked to get to Sheikh Jassim. He mentioned several names of dignitaries.

THE WEJBA BATTLE AS REPORTED BY A CONTEMPORARY HISTORIAN

The historian Nassir Jouher Al-Khairi talked about the Wejba Battle as follows:

> In the year 1893, Hafidh Pasha the Governor of Al-Ahsa'a used the opportunity of some Arabs transgressing on caravans passing through Al-Ahsa'a to attack Qatar in order to annex it to his Governorate. He requested from the Supreme Government to relieve Jassim from his post as District Administrator of Qatar and to capture him to send him to Basra from which to send him to Istanbul.

> Hafidh Pasha took some soldiers from Al-Ahsa'a to Qatar. Jassim fought them and defeated them.

This event instigated the Governor of Basra and became keener to get Jassim. The Governor of Basra sent 2 warships with 400 Ottoman soldiers to blockade Qatar. He also ordered Hafidh Pasha to proceed by land toward Qatar. The latter took with him about 700 soldiers. The armies reached Qatar at the same time. They arrested Ahmad, Sheikh Jassim's brother with several of Qatar's dignitaries and sent them to the warship hand cupped. Sheikh Jassim camped outside the country in about 5 miles. Sheikh Jassim sent to the Turkish leader of the Army asking for reconciliation to avoid bloodshed of the Muslims. The leader refused and went on to fight Jassim in order to kill or capture him. At that time, British warships arrived and offered Jassim their help in return for making Qatar under their protection. Jassim, the honorable man, refused the British help, turning to Allah to assist him in his tribulation. He fought the Turks with his Arabian tribes to defend their country. He won the war leaving about 400 dead and injured men, captured score of men and the rest fled on land or to the ship. Hafidh Pasha agreed to have peace, both sides released their captivities and everything went back to normal. Unfortunately, this was how the Turkish leaders treated the loyal Arabs.

All what happened did not change the heart of Sheikh Jassim toward the Turks. He continued to respect them as if nothing had happened.

The reader may wonder why we looked at this incident from several points of view. In the first place, it is very important in the history of Qatar; secondly, it shows how decision making was done by the Ottomans, and every storyteller had his interest in hiding some parts of the story and emphasizing others. It should be noted that we do not mean they all were liars nor that they were telling the whole truth. Every person involved in an incident looks at it differently. The reader may have heard of the story of two prisoners who looked from the window of the prison after it had finished raining. One said, "What a mess the rain did." The other looked at the sky saying how beautiful the sky looked after the rain (Carnegie).

VIEWS OF THE POLITICAL AND MILITARY OUTCOMES

There was ambiguity and suspicion with regard to Hafidh Pasha's attack on Qatar. It was originally to restore security in Nejd and punish the thieves in response to the Nejd merchants who sent their complaint to the government. Hafidh Pasha turned his attention to Qatar and Sheikh Jassim.

The important pertaining question is, what was the relation between Sheikh Jassim and the unlawful activities of robbery in Nejd? The Ottoman authorities in Nejd and Al-Ahsa'a did not secure the roads and punished the outlaws and blamed Sheikh Jassim for the problem. The merchants of Nejd pinpointed the persons and their tribes who were responsible for the insecurity in the roads. Why cram Sheikh Jassim's name in these activities?

The British officials in the Gulf region tried all they could to bring Sheikh Jassim to their side to infiltrate in the Arabian Peninsula, but they failed because he stayed firm against their threats or temptations. Hence, they found some weak and corrupt personalities among the Ottoman officials in the area that could listen to the rumors about Sheikh Jassim. The British made it easier for those Ottoman officials to accept the rumors by sending a complaint to the Ottoman government. Besides, there were some opportunists in the area who found their interests would be served best by getting rid of Sheikh Jassim.

The core of the problem was the corruption of the Ottoman officials, their inability to distinguish between the truth from the unfounded rumors, and their ignorance of the social and political situation in the Arabian Peninsula. The Qatar incident was exactly what happened in the Dara'iya incident in the early nineteenth century, when many innocent people were killed based on an unfounded rumor.

The Wejba Battle made it possible to establish direct communication with the sultan. Sheikh Jassim sent his well-written letter to the sultan. In that letter, Sheikh Jassim put his wisdom and shrewdness in selecting its wording to be convincing to the sultan. His aim was to stop the attempt of Hafidh Pasha from getting more troops to destroy Qatar, killing more people from both sides and overthrowing Sheikh Jassim from his legal post. If it were not for this letter, with Allah's decision, nobody can tell what would have happened to the future of Qatar. Besides, the dignitaries and chiefs of tribes of Qatar recognized the dangerous situation when they accompanied Sheikh Ahmad and stuck with him until the victory. Sheikh Jassim came out of the incident as a renowned leader in deciding the future of Qatar and the region.

Sheikh Jassim, with his truthfulness and calmness, was able to manage the events in accurate steps toward his victory, believing Allah would guide him every minute, and he was sure that he did not aggress on anybody. Therefore, he got even what he never thought would happen. Besides, he made good a military decision to use Wejba Fortress as his protective garrison for it was too far from the sea to be reached by the governor's bombing. Sheikh Jassim did not use his victory against the troops who had no choice but to obey the leader. He helped the soldiers to get to the ship where Hafidh Pasha was hiding. Some other soldiers went to Al-Ahsa'a, guarded by Jassim's men.

While Sheikh Jassim showed good manners to get the event behind him, we see Hafidh Pasha requested reinforcement to attack again. He found himself defeated so that he begged for reconciliation. What made Sheikh Jassim very angry was the arrest of his brother Ahmad and the other Qatar dignitaries by Hafidh Pasha, who gave them immunity but broke his promise. It was against the manners and traditions Sheikh Jassim had been accustomed to through his devotion to Islam. The intrigue and conspiracies against Sheikh Jassim had gone for quite some time to get rid of him, though changing the views of the center of decision in Istanbul was the goal of several parties.

Qatar, the stable entity, stood against the British desire to take it over as long as it was under the rule of Sheikh Jassim. The Ottoman Cabinet refused to change Sheikh Jassim because of his status and importance in Qatar and Al-Ahsa'a and their surroundings. According to the former governor of Basra, Mohammed Nafith Pasha, who received a request from A'akif, the district administrator of Nejd, to fire Sheikh Jassim from his post, Nafith Pasha recommended Sheikh Jassim to be given a medal for merit from the sultan before the visit of Nafith Pasha to Qatar in 1888.

If we go back to the outcome of the Wejba incident, we look at the summary of the minutes of the meeting held in the Istanbul January 20, 1893:

After receiving the report of the governor of Basra and the letter from Sheikh Jassim, the Cabinet decided to wrong the Basra governor Hafidh Pasha and found Sheikh Jassim innocent as he had no intention to do what happened. We took into consideration his conduct during the last twenty years of bringing Qatar peacefully and voluntarily to the Ottoman Empire. The report also had some references against Sheikh Jassim due to the rumors that were spread prior to the Hafidh Pasha's expedition to Qatar. The report blamed the governor of Basra, and he was fired from his job because he did not use wisdom in handling the problem. He created a problem with the person who had been the most respected in the region according to the Ottoman employees in the region.

They decided to form an investigating committee at a high level consisting of one of the leaders of the army, the chief of Basra nobles, Sa'eed Afandi, and the district administrator of Kuwait or his brother. We can say that what was discussed in the meeting and the report of the investigating committee was the border between the two eras of Qatar's history. While Hafidh Pasha's plan of getting rid of Sheikh Jassim and annexing Qatar to his governorate was blown in the wind, the people of Qatar breathed the air of peace and security. The opportunists and desirous men who were hoping to cash in on the removal of Sheikh Jassim suffered from frustration and disappointment. In fact, some of these men tried to convince some of the tribes to stay away from the conflict to be safe until they see who would win.

Some tribesmen and their leaders participated in the military expedition on the side of Hafidh Pasha and gave it an Arabian coverage for some money even though they knew that they were siding with corrupt Ottoman officers against a well-known Arab leader. Hence, this incident exposed the opportunists from the wise and loyal. Also Sheikh Jassim's star was glared in spite of the fabrications and conspiracies of his anomies. He was granted full authority over Qatar, which led to its independence.

* * *

CHAPTER 8

SHEIKH JASSIM PREOCCUPIED THE CALIPHATE

THE INCIDENT OF KUWAIT AND THE

CONNIVANCE OF BASRA GOVERNORATE

Let us first state that we are talking here about the controversies and even wars between countries like Kuwait, Qatar, Bahrain, and Abu Dhabi in history. After that came an era of goodwill and friendly feeling between these entities. There was some antagonism among leaders who were Arabs and Muslims as well as they were under the umbrella of the Ottoman Empire. The incident we are referring here to is what happened in Kuwait that led to the resignation of Sheikh Jassim and, ultimately, the end of the Ottoman rule in Qatar and Kuwait.

It has been proven through the succession of events that Sheikh Jassim was not a transgressor nor did he have any greed in taking over Kuwait as the Ottoman governors accused sheikhs of Arabian tribes. He had great forces of the Arabian tribes that gathered around him to take over Kuwait if it was his intention. But his goal was a noble one in standing for those whose rights were jeopardized.

The inheritors of Sheikh Mohammed Al-Sabah, the district administrator of Kuwait, and his brother Jarrah, after being assassinated, went to Sheikh Jassim, asking to help them get their rights. They accused the youngest brother, Sheikh Mubarak, of killing both the amir and his brother. Sheikh Jassim immediately contacted the supreme government in Istanbul about the incident and told them that he was determined to get the rights of the inheritors at any cost. He was enthused with the Arabian gallantry to assist those who came to solicit his help. But the governor of Basra, A'arif Pasha, and the military leader Lieutenant General Mohsen Pasha accused someone else and ordered to give the job to Mubarak. They praised him to the supreme government. At the same time, they propagated rumors against Sheikh Jassim, who was getting ready to march to Kuwait.

The Special Council of Deputies in Istanbul met on November 23, 1898, to discuss what should be done administratively and militarily according to the report received from Sheikh Jassim. The council approved the appointment of Mubarak Al-Sabah, honorary district administrator of Kuwait. It also decided to send a military force to prevent Sheikh Jassim from invading Kuwait. The Council's members believed that whatever Sheikh Jassim's intention and goals, his invasion of Kuwait might create tribal disobedience. The Council continued to prepare for sending eight battalions under the leadership of Mohsen Pasha to Kuwait based on what Sheikh Jassim was trying to do.

The reason for sending military forces was that Sheikh Jassim proceeded to do what was not within the authority he was assigned for. Besides, this move might lead to tribal war. His telegram that he sent included that. We are afraid that this incident could become a precedent in the future for his move too.

On the other hand, the act of assassination of which Mubarak Al-Sabah was accused that led to the complaint of the hires of the assassinated sheikhs required sending a military force to make the investigations and spread security and stability in the area. We are awaiting the decision of the Sultan.

The sultan issued a decree based on the memorandum sent by the prime minister on the appointment of Mubarak Al-Sabah, who was accused of killing his two brothers, as district administrator. Hence, Sheikh Jassim led his tribesmen to attack Kuwait. He camped at the gate called Oraij, about twenty-five hours from Qatar. A'arif Pasha, the governor of Basra, and Mohsen Pasha, the army commander, sent a telegram to Istanbul telling their government about the move of Sheikh Jassim in order to restore the rights of the hires of the assassinated sheikhs. Although the latter submitted a complaint to the government, no one listened to them. The governor and the commander ordered the administrator of Al-Ahsa'a to cut the water and supplies from Sheikh Jassim's group. They also sent a memorandum to the administrator of Nejd telling him what to do so that security would prevail there:

> We need to get the decree of appointing Mubarak as the District Administrator of Kuwait and the protection of the rights of the hires Mohammed and Jarrah Al-Sabah to speed up solving the problem. It is necessary to send 8 Battalions to Qatar and inform Sheikh Jassim to stop his movements and all actions contrary to the desire of the Sultan or he would be responsible for what would happen. We are waiting for your instructions. Signed and delivered December 4, 1898.

The Special Council of Deputies held a meeting on December 6, 1898, after receiving the telegram from A'arif Pasha and Mohsen Pasha and decided the following:

The Council suggested Hassan Pasha, a member of the Supreme Council of the Empire, to undertake the investigation job because of his great knowledge on Iraqi affairs. The council went into the details of what happened at the assassination of the amir of Kuwait and his brother and Sheikh Jassim's approaching Kuwait. It also mentioned that the foreign embassies began to discuss the incident.

If the Council sends Hassan Pasha to Basra, which is far away from Qatar, the investigation may take three to four months. For the current local situation and the urgency of the matter, the Council decided to dispatch a telegram to Sheikh Jassim to warn him of his recent movements and give Mohsen Pasha the military forces to lead them to Kuwait immediately to protect the region from any unforeseen events. The Council decided to put away the appointment of Mubarak Al-Sabah, the district administrator of Kuwait. The suit against Mubarak of accusing him of the assassinating his brothers should be thoroughly investigated in accordance with the Islamic codes and civil laws and treat him justly and accordingly.

The movement of the military forces to Kuwait should be kept secret. They should pretend that they were coming to stop Sheikh Jassim. When the army arrives at Kuwait, the commander should immediately start the legal proceedings of the assassination on one hand, and prevent Sheikh Jassim from entering Kuwait on the other hand. The Ministry of Interior has been informed of the situation in the governorate of Basra. The final decision is with the sultan.

The Reason for the Crisis

The conduct of Sheikh Jassim was within a normal administrative course of action. He sent a telegram to the sultan explaining what happened and what he intended to do. The following is what he mentioned in his telegram dated January 27, 1899:

> We are not disobedient or rebellious in any meaning of these words. We are not acting except to what confirm with the Sultan's policy. I have served the Empire all this time with my effort and money without thinking of any reward. All what happened was that Hameed and Jarrah, the orphans of the assassinated Amir of Kuwait and his brother for no legitimate reason came to me asking for help. Hence, I thought that it was my duty to present the case to you.
>
> His Excellency the Commander of the Sixth Sultan army received large sum of money from

Mubarak Al-Sabah. Therefore, he purified Mubarak and recommended him to be the Amir. Hence, Mubarak caused damaging to the Empire through his tricks and conspiracies in addition to what he had done to these orphans. These actions aroused my conscious and my loyalty to the Empire to restore the rights of these orphans and save the Government the cost of doing this job. As long as Mubarak is the District Administrator of Kuwait, he shall continue harming the Empire and deprive the rights of the orphans. Besides, these orphans will never be safe from his aggression on their lives as he did with their fathers.

Obviously, there should be a military division in Kuwait to restore peace and security by a new District Administrator after the dismissal of Mubarak. Therefore, Kuwait will be back into the Empire with sound administration.

The minister of foreign affairs sent a memorandum to the prime minister about the subject as follows:

To his Excellency the Prime Minister, there are 150 soldiers of the British ground forces were moved from Bombay to the Gulf of Oman. They sent three warships to the waters of Masqat. Although, they wrote in the newspapers that these movements were to show strength in front of the Iranians after the assassination of an Iranian tele-graph employee by local people. But this is the declared reason. However, we believe that Sheikh Mohammed bin Ali bin Ibrahim, the opponent of Mubarak Al-Sabah, had something to do with the British movements. Sheikh Mohammed was the Deputy District Administrator to the former Amir of Kuwait. Besides, Sheikh Yusuf, the nephew of Sheikh Mohammed, fled to Basra then went to Qatar to start the movement of disobedience. We enclosed, herewith, the full investigation from Shah Bender and Bombay.

Sheikh Jassim, the Center of Events

Thus the Ottoman Empire and the British as well as the Arabian tribes had a new event to keep them occupied with Sheikh Jassim being the main subject of the discussion. The Ottoman Cabinet held a meeting on February 18, 1899, with the chair being Prime Minister Ria'at Pasha. The meeting issued the following memorandum:

The members listened to the memorandum sent by the Minister of Foreign Affairs and its enclosures. They also listened to the translation of Sheikh Jassim's telegram. It is believed that the British movements were not as it was stated in the newspapers, but could have something to do with the local sheikhs. It is noted that Sheikh Jassim had responded to the complaint of the orphans who were not treated fairly in Basra, but sided with Mubarak who was accused of assassinating the Amir of Kuwait and confiscated his wealth. This indicates that Sheikh Jassim had acted on behalf of the Ottoman Government. If there was good handling with wisdom of the event from the beginning, Sheikh Jassim would not have moved toward Kuwait. Besides, Sheikh Jassim had suggested in his telegram to dismiss Mubarak from his post so that Kuwait would remain under the rule of the Empire. The information that came from Shah Bender with respect to Sheikh Mohammed Ibrahim, former Deputy of the Amir, being in Bombay with the British raise an alarm and present the Ottoman Empire as being unable to solve the problem. In order to avoid further deterioration of the problem, there must be military forces to be sent to Kuwait after the dismissal of Mubarak from his administrative post and being trialed on the accusation of assassination and confiscation so that the problem will be dealt with once and for all. It is remained to find the way of bringing Mubarak to Basra through intersession of the chief of the nobles in Basra to mediate between Mubarak and Sheikh Jassim.

On the other hand, although several meetings were held in Istanbul on high levels, no step was taken toward a solution. There were five battalions brought to Basra five months before intended to go to Nejd that were ready to be sent to Kuwait even though the soldiers had been living in tents and were tired especially of the weather of Basra, unfamiliar to them.

The sons of the assassinated amir of Kuwait and his brother sent a telegram to the prime minister. They stated that obviously the gathering of troops in Basra was illusive pretention of protecting Mubarak from Sheikh Jassim's attack. Mubarak, who had been freed from his accusation of assassinating our fathers and being appointed amir, believed that these troops were to help him. However, he did not thank the caliph but began to arm the people of Kuwait and its tribes to fight those whom he thought were opposing him. Such an action would certainly lead to the loss of hundreds of lives and create unnecessary turmoil. It was signed by Sabah and Saud on April 3, 1899.

According to this telegram, the commander of the army, Ridha Pasha, directed by the prime minister, sent a telegram to the marshalcy of the sixth army on April 5, 1899, stating that the sons of the assassinated amir and his brother had confirmed that Mubarak Al-Sabah had armed the people of Kuwait by force and attacked tribes a few days ago. You should take every action to prevent any development of such an act.

The marshalcy of the sixth army not only denied the claims of these orphans but also overturned the impression the government had completely in the telegram reply on April 8, 1899, as follows:

> We do not need to repeat what we had said before to waste your time. Mubarak Al-Sabah did not make such move against the caravans or the cities nor did he transgress over anyone. Even if he has the intention and determination against Sheikh Jassim, Qatar is 150 hours on land away from Kuwait which means we would have noticed that. If some of the tribes that use the looting and plundering as way of life or those tribes that reside near Qatar came close to Kuwait, his move is quite normal. As to the orphans, they are young rich boys do not know the nature of the bedwin way of life. Besides, there are some corrupt lawyers are taking advantage of the situation to falsify the news. Therefore, we do not see any need to investigate. The truth is as we present it to you.

In this telegram that was sent from Basra governorate, Hmoud Al-Sabah, Mubarak's brother, indicated the recovery of the herds and other movable assets taken during the raid. He also mentioned that Mubarak went to those tribes for reconciliation after the few losses of life. The marshalcy of the sixth army added that they did not notice any sign of Mubarak being against the Ottoman Empire as indicated by the telegram sent from the orphans Sabah and Saud. As for the raids between the tribes, it was quite normal among the bedouins. We should note that the claims against Mubarak were originally the antagonism between Mubarak and Yusuf Al-Ibrahim. It was signed by Lieutenant General Mohsen and acting governor Jamal.

The reader may notice the controversy between the views of the problem. This is due, as Sheikh Jassim mentioned in his telegram to the sultan, to the corruption of the high-ranked Ottoman officials. Apparently, Mubarak Al-Sabah knew that he had no chance of being the amir of Kuwait. He also had great wealth through his investment in the pearl industry. He killed the amir and the next-in-line brother. He knew that he could bribe the commander of the army and the governor of Basra to stand in his side and recommend him to be the amir. However, he was not a good politician or even smart enough to play safe by embracing his nephews, promising them to be next in line to be the amir, asking Yusuf Al-Ibrahim to continue being his deputy and claiming to be looking for the assassin. But what he did was to fight everybody except the governor and the commander in Basra.

Sheikh Jassim received the attention of the caliph more than anybody else. But Lieutenant General Mohsen and the governor of Basra were successful in turning the case upside down and deceived the high-ranked government about Mubarak Al-Sabah.

THE SHARIF OF MECCA GIVES HIS VIEW

This is another view of a religiously respectable person about the Kuwaiti crisis. The sharif of Mecca, A'oun Al-Rafiq, wrote three years later the following:

> To the Sultan: The District Administrator of Kuwait Mubarak bin Sabah is a feebleminded man. He killed his oldest brother who was the Amir of Kuwait and the other brother. But Mohsen Pasha and the Governor of Basra declared against the truth that assassin was someone else. They also praised Mubarak and recommended him to be the District Administrator. Mubarak is known to be an enemy of the Empire. He conspired with the Captain of the British warship that passed by Kuwait to buy British weapons

and ammunition at very low prices to be sold to the bedwins in Nejd and Hejaz. These bedwins used the weapons in illegal activities. Moreover, since he is treacherous, he forced some tribes of Kuwait to migrate to the Arabian Peninsula and the Iranian coasts to get money from them in dubious ways to give the Pasha we referred to thousands of liras to get him on his side.

As long as the Mohsen Pasha is in Basra, Mubarak Al-Sabah will continue to sell the bedwins of Nejd and Hejaz weapons. If he is let alone, the British will, God forbid, take over Kuwait and ultimately insecurity and disturbance will prevail in Iraq, Nejd and Hejaz. Since Mubarak has no support or influence among his people, none of the tribes follow him except his servants. It is necessary to send a force of fifty men to apprehend him and send him to Basra, issue an order for me to the job or send Sultan's soldiers to take care of him and appoint someone else in his post. It is also necessary to establish a custom office to get revenues for the treasury. I wanted to inform you as a loyal subject of the Islamic Nation. It is signed by A'oun Al-Rafiq, Amir Mecca, dated August 21, 1902.

Two years later, Amir Mecca A'oun Al-Rafiq sent another letter to the Sultan as follows:

The District Administrator of Kuwait Mubarak bin Sabah attacked the District of A'aridh with some bedwins from Iraq and Nejd and took over it. He supported Abdul Rahman bin Faisal Al-Saud to become A'aridh's Amir. Mubarak advanced later on toward the region under the control of bin Rasheed. The sides collided in a battle which led to the defeat of Mubarak who returned home. In the battle there were 3000 bedwins died. A'aridh remained under the control of Abdul Rahman Al-Saud.

District is located east of Nejd. Its center is Riyadh and it is about 60 hours from the coast of the Gulf. Mubarak was sending arms and money to Ibn Saud regularly. Hence, Ibn Saud may gain strength so that he will defeat Ibn Rasheed and go under the protection of the British like Mubarak did. In order to avoid such thing to happen, Ibn Rasheed should be delegated the authority to fight Ibn Saud and provided with the necessary assistance from the Sultan. I think this is necessary because Nejd is bordered with Hejaz. This is what motivated me to present these ideas. Please put these situations forward to the Sultan as soon as possible.

Our presentation of these discussions and ideas of different authorities in the region was to give the reader a complete picture of what happened even though they are not directly related to Qatar and Sheikh Jassim. These events indicate that the Ottoman Empire lost its control over its territories, and the corruption has spread over its high officials. Otherwise, how could someone like Mubarak not only get away with murdering his two brothers but control a small entity, Kuwait, from which he played a big role in Nejd? Besides, the central government could send great military forces, but it was unable to control its own subordinate officials in governorates.

It should be noted that the Kuwaiti incident gave the personality of Sheikh Jassim a big boost. The orphans of the amir of Kuwait and his brother could not find any shoulder to cry on except Sheikh Jassim. They sent telegrams to Basra and Istanbul, but no one was listening. Sheikh Jassim brought their case to the sultan and the prime minister and led troops to the border of Kuwait. His reputation with the sultan led the councils of deputies and ministers to keep on meeting about the problem.

The Ottoman Flag Left Qatar

No one has ever noted that the existence of the Ottomans as an occupying force or military invasion is the case with the Ottoman territorial entities. It was symbolic presence with very limited influence in running the country by Sheikh Jassim. For example, the German traveller was hesitant to take pictures without the permission from Sheikh Jassim as being advised by the Ottoman garrison. Hence, the Ottomans were expected to leave Qatar. There were two events that led the Ottomans to leave Qatar: the Al-Wejba incident, which we have discussed in details earlier, and the market incident.

The Market Incident

As we mentioned earlier, the Ottomans had a battalion in Qatar, which had no control over the administration of Qatar. People of Qatar, however, used to watch the soldiers carefully because they were not accustomed to having foreign forces in their territory. One day, there were about twelve soldiers and a first lieutenant walking in the market when they saw an Iranian and an Arabian fighting. The soldiers interfered, then they started to beat both fighters. When people saw what the soldiers were doing, they attacked the soldiers. Consequently, the officer was injured, and two civilians were killed and three injured. The fight was only with knives, sticks, and rocks. The soldiers ran away back to their fortress.

People rushed to get their guns and surrounded the fortress from all sides and started to shoot at the fortress for about half an hour. The soldiers, however, did not respond. The Qataris demanded the surrender of the two killers to apply the Islamic rules against them. The two soldiers were given to the people of Qatar, who chained them, awaiting the authorization of the Ottoman authority to try them. Meanwhile, the soldiers compensated those who claimed loss of merchandise during the fight. The Qatari were not satisfied with that; they cut off water from the fortress and prevented the soldiers from leaving the fortress.

The commander of the battalion sent letter to the Basra governorate on March 31, 1899. But according to the chief commander and the acting governor, they did not receive any letter about the incident until April 24. They informed the government in Istanbul about the incident. The government in Istanbul appointed Anees Pasha governor of Basra as a first step. The new governor sent a telegram to the ministry of interior on April 30 based on the letters that came from Nejd April 13 as follows:

> According to the suggestion of Ahmad, Sheikh Jassim's brother, which was sent through SS *Mejdersan* to calm down the people of Qatar and appoint Deputy Administrator for Qatar, the battalion Major went to Sheikh Ahmad's house. The Major assured Sheikh Ahmad to get permission to punish the two soldiers who were accused of killing the Qatari man, return the stolen stuff, pay money to people who were injured and prevent soldiers from leaving the fortress. Besides, Sheikh Ahmad demanded that the Ottoman Government should send two persons; a military and a civilian to investigate the incidence so that people of Qatar will calm down. Accordingly, the reason for the incidence and the way it ended, led the Ministry of Interior to investigate the incidence where it happened and the advice of how to prevent similar incidence from happening. Besides, the Chief Commander Mohsen Pasha believed that after this incidence, there would be no friendly coexistence between the soldiers and the people of Qatar possible.

It was also believed that Major Rassoul, the commander of the battalion, became so old that his decision in that incident was unacceptable militarily. Hence, the existence of the battalion became liable for further incidents to occur. It should be noted that the time for changing the battalion became near. The ministry of interior sent a telegram to the governor of Basra, Anees Pasha, on May 2, 1899. The latter replied two days later with the following telegram:

> Today a man came to me from Sheikh Ahmad delivering a letter from the people of Qatar in which they complain about the unacceptable behavior of the battalion stationed in Qatar. The carrier of the letter told me that Sheikh Jassim was about 5 to 6 hours from the incidence when it happened. The quarrel was not planned ahead of time but it took place accidently. There was no other incidence happened after that. It resulted into antagonism between the soldiers and the people of Qatar. The incidence was reported to the Nejd Governorate as was reported to the high authorities and the Ministry of Interior. Since it became hard to bring the two factions together, we are awaiting your decision. May 4, 1899.

The commander of the Sixth Army looked at the incident from a different angle. He thought that it was a premeditated movement and planned a trap aimed at getting rid of the Ottoman battalion from Qatar. He indicated in a telegram sent May 9 in response to a telegram sent to him on May 5. His telegram stated the following:

> The Caliph knows that the information sent by employees like those in Qatar can be untrue or not precise. You should know that Jassim AL-Thani always caused trouble and attempt to do harm in the District of Nejd. The procedures you have taken without precautions or deep con-

siderations were for peace security. However, Jassim and people of Qatar tried their utmost to remove the Ottoman battalion from their area and confiscate modern weapons.

The telegram I sent April 23 describing what the battalion had to suffer from the attack on it can be considered the basis of what happened. Therefore, the new battalion that we shall send to replace the existing one will have to face the same trouble. It is necessary to send the Naqeeb of Basra (The most respected person who was chosen as the chief of dignitaries) and the officer Shamil Bieg to Qatar to investigate the incidence according to the instruction of the Caliph. I am waiting for your further instruction to send the new battalion.

After all these communications, the Council of Deputies held a meeting on May 27 to decide.

According to the telegrams and reports sent from Basra governorate indicating that the battalion and the people of Qatar, the movements of Sheikh Jassim, the telegram sent by the commander of the Sixth Army and other communications, taking into consideration principles and wisdom of the Caliph, the Council decided to move the battalion stationed between Basra and Umarah because of the hot weather and it became unnecessary. The council then described the incident as was mentioned earlier. The current battalion had to be replaced with another one with a more efficient major. Since Sheikh Jassim had been a troublemaker in the district of Nejd and the new battalion could face the same problem as its predecessor, the Naqeeb of Basra and the officer Shamil had to go ahead with their mission of investigation.

It should be noted that the Naqeeb of Basra told us that he was ready to go to meet Sheikh Jassim in Qatar, carrying with him a letter of his investigating task. He was accompanied by the officer Shamil.

The plan was submitted to the caliph together with all the communications referred to earlier.

It should be noted that the market incident speeded up the departure of the Ottoman's presence in Qatar. The incident became the last event that occurred that resulted into changing the relation between the Ottomans and the people of Qatar. It also indicated the good gesture of the sultan and his kindness in solving the problem the best way, bypassing the unfounded claims of the Sixth Army commander.

Thus, the findings of the Naqeeb of Basra indicated the clearance of the name of Sheikh Jassim. The Naqeeb was neutral in his investigation, unaffected by the exaggeration of the Sixth Army commander and his hatred of Sheikh Jassim. The investigation mentioned that Sheikh Jassim had been playing an important role in the peace and security of Nejd District. The fact-finding committee recommended replacing the major in charge of the battalion.

POLITICAL INGENUITY: THE USE OF RESIGNATION

The resignation of Sheikh Jassim had been a resort to free him from the adherence to the unwarranted command of authorities as well as to guide Qatar toward its independence. He used this method, whether with the Ottoman government or the other foreign powers or local sheikhs. When Sheikh Jassim became furious, he resigned from his post with calculated risk to regain his position and became stronger after his resignation was refused. His resignation was not meant to be withdrawal or to give up his long accomplishments of getting the tribes together under his leadership. He delegated his leadership to his brother Sheikh Ahmad and left claiming that he had become too old to run his entity.

One can look at Sheikh Jassim's resignation as a way of personal pride and to indicate that he was not in need of any position that gave no income but headache. Since he was able to bring together all the tribes of Qatar under his leadership, he did not need those corrupt Ottoman employees to secure his leadership. Although Sheikh Jassim was the district administrator of Qatar officially, he threw the responsibility in the lap of his brother Sheikh Ahmad after the Wejba incident. The governor of Basra, Anees Pasha, referred to such an arrangement in his telegram sent on June 30 to the prime minister in which he said the following:

> Among the communications we received as replies to our advices and commands that we sent to Nejd and Sheikh Jassim, that the latter was submissive to the command and ruling of the Caliph. He would not do anything, or his brother Sheikh Ahmad who is running the affairs of Qatar except what would please the Caliph. While he was giving these assurances, he brought the complaint against Mubarak Al-Sabah who was anti-Ottoman Empire . . . Sheikh Jassim seemed to mention in every letter that the administration of Qatar was given to his brother Sheikh Ahmad and that he had never sent any telegram to the Ministry of Interior. We have noticed that Sheikh Ahmad has good characters and in good terms with Sheikh Jassim, Therefore, we recommend to give the District Administration Office to Sheikh Ahmad. The matter as always is in the hands of the Caliph.

Sheikh Jassim announced his resignation because of his old age, but some other time because he was sick. Since he mentioned his brother as the caretaker of the Qatar administrative affairs, he told the Ottoman officials to replace him with his brother. After the last petition of his resignation that Sheikh Jassim sent to the governor of Basra, Anees Pasha, in mid 1899, he mentioned the following:

> It is known to you that I submitted my resignation from the District Administration of Qatar since you visited us. But it was not accepted. I believe my resignation was mainly because I

was unable to bring together the pleasure of the Supreme Authority and the distrust and conspiracy of some officials in Government. Therefore, I request from your Excellency accepting my resignation as soon as my petition reaches you. You may appoint whoever you think fits and send him to take my place.

If you ask about the reasons for my resignation, they are many; first the reason I told about several times. The second is the Zibara incidence (market incidence). The third is the problem with Sheikh Mubarak Al-Sabah who assassinated his two older brothers and confiscated the property of their sons. The latters submitted petitions to get their rights, but there was no response. When we tried to draw the attention to the problem, the corrupt administrators in Basra reversed the facts because they received briberies from Mubarak . . .

It seems from the aforementioned that the resignation was the result of Sheikh Jassim's feelings of despair. This was the first time that Sheikh Jassim did not mention his brother Sheikh Ahmad as a possible replacement but left it to the governor to select a person. This emphasizes the condition he was in as well as his relation with the Ottoman officials. However, he knew that the Ottoman government could not appoint anyone without his approval because Sheikh Jassim was the richest and most influential in Qatar. His generosity and strong personality made the tribes of Qatar submissive to him.

The problem for the Ottoman government was that if they accepted Sheikh Jassim's resignation, they had to appoint someone he approved of. Hence, according to the information received from the governor of Basra and the commander of the Sixth Army, the Deputy Council discussed Sheikh Jassim's resignation on July 15, 1899, to decide the following:

We have received note from the Commander of the Sixth Army suggesting to send military force from Basra to punish the District Administrator of Qatar because his disobedience and conspiracy reached unacceptable level as he endangered the Ottoman battalion.

However, after the discussion of the matter and since Sheikh Jassim has been undoubtedly submissive to the orders of the Caliph, we see no reason to send any military force to Qatar. In accordance to the desire of the Sultan, there should be some efforts to settle the case without military action but the use of advice. We have received a reply from the Governorate of Basra which we read it together with the memorandum from the Ministry of Interior indicating some advices and information were sent to both the Administration of Nejd and Sheikh Jassim stating that the latter was submissive to the decision of the Sultan and he will not take any action that the Sultan will not approve. Besides, Sheikh Jassim brother who is the caretaker of Qatar, it is suggested that Sheikh Ahmad will be officially the District Administrator of Qatar as the resignation of Sheikh Jassim will be accepted. This will be communicated to the Governor of Basra.

Most of the people of Qatar got their substance directly or indirectly from Sheikh Jassim, who owned most of the pearl hunting or fish boats. They also considered him as their leader because he had brought them together in unity. Besides, Sheikh Jassim was known to be generous, kind to the needy, respectable, and having a strong personality. Therefore, the Council of Deputies could not bypass him as some other corrupt high-ranked officers or governors who tried to cover the sunlight with a sifter, as the Arabic saying goes. However, even the Council of Deputies planned to please Sheikh Jassim by accepting his resignation and appointing his brother Sheikh Ahmad in his place but thought of appointing an outsider when Sheikh Jassim would be out of the picture. They were naive in their thinking. Sheikh Ahmad held very good standing with the people of Qatar, not as Sheikh Jassim's brother but because of his good character, and had been running the administration of Qatar for several years. People had seen him in action and when he had been sacrificed to be imprisoned during the Wejba incident. Therefore, they would not accept any other person to replace him.

THE INDEPENDENCE OF QATAR

Finally, Sheikh Jassim was able to impose his political pressure to become part of the regional leadership after the withdrawal of the Ottoman Empire from the region. He was recognized as renowned leader in the area and the only authority in his entity.

It remains to point out the agreement between the Ottomans and the British, which included the recognition of the independence of Qatar, and that was tied with Sheikh Jassim and his family descendants. According to the desire of both the Ottoman Empire and Great Britain to agree on final decisions regarding all territories of the Arab Gulf and surrounding areas, there were meetings between the representative of the Ottoman Empire, the ex-prime minister Haqqi Pasha, and the representative of Great Britain, the foreign minister; we shall quote some articles that concern our subject:

QATAR

Article 11—The Ottoman Nejd District region whose northern border was indicated in Article 7 of this agreement will end at the Gulf at appoint cross from Zekhnonia Island, which belongs to that district. There will be a line that starts from the Gulf to the Empty Quarter in the south. This line will separate Qatar Peninsula from Nejd, as marked by a blue line on the attached map (folder A5). The Ottoman government has given up all its claims of Qatar Peninsula.

The two governments decided that the administration of this peninsula will be run by Sheikh Jassim and his heirs after him. The British government will make sure that the sheikh of Bahrain will not interfere in the internal affairs of Qatar as an independent entity.

Article 12—The people of Bahrain have the right to pass by Zekhnonia for fishing or staying as the situation permits before and during winter. There will be no additional taxes to be imposed on the people of Bahrain.

BAHRAIN

Article 13 —The Ottoman Empire will give up all rights concerning the Bahrain Islands including the two small islands, Upper Lebanon and Lower Lebanon. It recognizes Bahrain's independence. The British government will also indicate that it has no desire to include Bahrain as part of its territories.

Article 14—The British government declares in front of the Ottoman government no additional taxes will be taken by the sheikh of Bahrain from other pearl-picking people in the waters of Bahrain.

Article 15—The Bahrainis who reside in any Ottoman territories will be considered foreigners and can demand protection of British consulates. Those Bahrainis who had the privileges of being protected according to former agreements will be protected according to the European international laws.

THE GULF OF BASRA[9]* (THE ARAB GULF)

Article 16—In order for the British government to protect its interest and as a humanitarian gesture as well as to insure the adherence to maritime laws by those using international waters, it took some measures and arrangements, which the Ottoman government

---

[9] · Great Britain agreed to the name the Gulf of Basra, yet it kept referring to it later as the Persian Gulf.

should recognize in the Gulf of Basra. These arrangements are as follows:

- Procedures of navigating, turning on lights, and installing Bouygues and encouraged facilities;
- having maritime police; and
- procedures of quarantine.
- The Ottoman government will keep its rights over the coasts and the territorial waters of the entities under its control.

THE COMMITTEE OF FIXING THE BORDERS

Article 17—The two governments agreed to appoint representatives to affix the borders according to Articles 5, 7, and 10 of this agreement on ground and draw a detailed sketch of these borders with a written explanation to be an appendix to this agreement. All these documents must be signed by the representatives of both sides.

Article 18—This agreement will be signed, and documents will be exchanged in London as soon as possible and within no more than three months. The two heads of the delegates have already signed the agreement and put their seals on it. The agreement was written in London on July 29, 1913.

There were some appendices to the agreement, as well as a secret appendix containing definitions and declaration of Qatar's independence.

> The Ottoman Government defines the term *Kuwait issues* to mean internal as well as foreign issues. However, the Sheikh of Kuwait has no right of signing any agreement other than within this Agreement. The Kuwaiti boundaries as well as those of Qatar have been set and self-rule has been granted. Orders were issued to all Ottoman employees and soldiers to leave the lands of these entities.

The British Government recognizes the decision taken by the Ottoman Government with respect to the Zekhnonia Island as part of Nejd District. Hence, it will give the Sheikh of Bahrain 1,000 British Lira as compensation for him giving up that Island which is very close to Nejd coast.

These appendices were signed in two copies by the heads of delegates.

SUMMARY AND CONCLUSION

PREFACE

In this section we shall review in short first the emergence and development of the Ottoman Empire. Secondly, the evolution of Qatar from scattered tribes to a tribal federation then to a country with the role of Sheikh Jassim bin Thani as its leader toward an independent country. The final part will be devoted to Sheikh Jassim as a person, as a leader of its people, and as a distinguished Arab of charisma.

THE OTTOMAN EMPIRE

The following are the main aspects of the Ottoman Empire:

First—the Ottoman Empire started on Allah's piety and Islamic principles and goals to spread the oneness of God and that Mohammed is Allah's servant and messenger. All these came in the will of Prince Othman the First to his son Orkhan (1326–1350) while he was dying, saying,

> O' my son you must adhere to the honorable religion of Islam and consult its knowledgeable sheikhs in everything you are about to do. You must be generous to people and respect them as

they deserve. Honor the knowledgeable sheikhs among them. The best of people are those who are most beneficial to them. You must honor the order of Allah, be merciful to His creations and fight for His cause.

When Orkhan settled with his rule (1327) and issued its monetary unit, he made sure that it would be a declaration of an Islamic state. Hence, he put on one side "No God but Allah and Mohammed is His Messenger" surrounded by the names of the four Guided Caliphs, who followed the Prophet Mohammed. On the other side he inscribed his name, Orkhan. He made sure to make his army an instrument of war and guidance. That is why a group of Islamic jurisprudents consulted with them and guided the people. He had the position of military judge, one of the most prestigious posts during the entire Ottoman rule.

Second—The Ottoman state accomplished its role in advancing into Europe and was successful in taking over Constantinople, which was renamed by the Sultan Mohammed Al-Fatih (the conqueror) Islam Bole and spreading Islam in Europe. The Islamic caliphate became a great power in both the sea and on land. The Ottomans took over the Balkan entities. We see now Islam is still in Bosnia, Albania, and others. The Ottoman Empire was not only a strong power but also rich. France used to borrow from it occasionally. When the Ottoman military commander, Khairiddin Barbarossa, was in France, he demanded that the church bells should not be rung in Tollone. The French granted his request.

Third—All Ottoman caliphs and sultans kept great respect for Islam, built mosques, held prayers, and maintained the two sacred mosques in all the territories of their empire.

Fourth—The Ottoman caliphate emerged and spread through the west, arousing fear of the Crusaders. This empire began thirty-plus years after the downfall of Baghdad, which gave the Crusaders happiness. The latter's fear was warranted as the Ottoman army was advancing fast to reach Vienna. It was Allah's will to have Othman, the founder of the Ottoman Dynasty, who was born in the same year of the fall of Baghdad.

West Europe, Great Britain, France, Austria, and others were diligently working in secret and in the open together with Russia, using all possible means and ways to destroy the Ottoman Empire. While the British were maneuvering in the Arab Gulf, Arab Sea, and the Red Sea, Russia engaged in a war called the Crimean War. The secret Masonic and Zionist organizations infiltrated into the Muslim population under the banners of civilization, freedom, and democracy to change young men and women from Islam to secularism. Young men were offered scholarships to study in Western universities. The list can go on of the methods used to destroy the population from inside. When the British prime minister asked the Ottoman prime minister, Fo'ad Pasha, what is the strongest nation in the world? Fo'ad Pasha answered, "The Ottoman Empire, because you are trying to destroy it from the outside, and we are trying to destroy it from the inside, but none of us is successful."

Fifth—There was some bad conduct and mistakes done by officials including governors and high-ranked military officers. Some of these employees began to take bribes and gifts to favor criminals. Such corruption led to create gaps between people and the government to the extent of some tribal leaders or sheikhs resorting to foreign powers.

Sixth—Some of the wise Arab leaders, however, remain loyal to the Ottoman Empire rejecting repeated inducements by the British; a good example was Sheikh Jassim in spite of the plots and false reports submitted by corrupt high ranked officials.

Seventh—Unfortunately, when a governor and army commander fabricated reports to the central government in order to wage a war against Qatar, it was discovered they were wrong; no punishment was effected against them. Lives were lost, buildings were destroyed, and weapons and ammunitions were lost for nothing but personal antagonism. An example was the Wejba battle. Even the Midhat Pasha's campaign was not warranted such involvement of forces, tribes, and other civilians.

Eighth—The Ottoman Empire was for six centuries the guard for the Muslims and their defender against their enemies and invaders of their territories. It stood firm against all waves of the Crusaders, Persian Safavids, and the Russians. It is noticeable what happened to Muslim territories after the defeat of the Ottoman Empire and how the Muslims became subject to be divided among Western powers.

Ninth—Since the Arabs and their language were the essence of Islam, they should not be considered second-class citizens as the Ottoman governors and high-ranked officers did. This is by no means Islamic—to segregate against Muslims of other race, color, or place of origin. However, the Ottomans treated the Arabs as if they were inferior and occasionally referred to them as bedouins. That led the Arabs to interpret any movement from Ottoman officials as anti-Arab. They revolted several times. Besides, the Ottoman government used to send officials who had no idea of the Arabic culture and tradition.

Tenth—The change of government to the Etihad and Taraqi Party (Union and Progress Party), whose leader was Mustafa Ataturk, declared Turkey a secular state, changed the written language from Arabic letters to latten's and abolished all Islamic laws for European civil laws. These decisions created great resentment among Arab leaders and many Islam-adherent Turkish people. But the new leader, backed by young men and women, especially the learned ones, and advised by foreign anti-Islamic persons who had infiltrated into the country for such a purpose, succeeded in enforcing their new ideas.

Finally, we hope that historians and other researchers will undertake more studies as there is a huge number of documents in the archives of Turkey, England, Europe, and Arab countries awaiting diligent researchers.

QATAR

The peninsula of Qatar was considered a safe, remote refuge to several tribes that fled the cruel massacred of the Persian Safavids known as the destruction of Basra, or to those that came from the Arabian Peninsula because of severe drought or other reasons. Since these tribes were not closely related by blood, they were fighting with each other for any reason. Sheikh Mohammed bin Thani and his successor, Sheikh Jassim, tried diligently to bring together these tribes under the banner of Islam. Sheikh Jassim, who was known to have a strong personality, generosity, and religious adherence, was able to bring together those tribes under his leadership. He led Qatar to its independence. It was a long, bumpy road that he had to go through without bowing his head to foreigners or corrupt Ottoman administrators. During his sheikhdom, the district administrator or independent amir raised the banner of Islam very high, respected the good tribal tradition, and cared for his people as father to his sons. He welcomed his people in his palace regardless of their income or social status. He used to give the sermon every Friday.

<<Photo #5>>
Sheikh Jassim's Palace and Mosque

Throughout the book, we have gone through the historical and political development during the eighteenth and nineteenth centuries, especially when the Ottomans emerged as a great power in the world and in the Arab Gulf region. They expelled the Portuguese, who tortured the Muslims residents of the Gulf coast and confiscated trading ships passing through the Arab Gulf and Arabian Sea.

We discussed briefly the geographical, social, and economic conditions in Qatar to show that in spite of its poor conditions, it was the center of attention to the Ottomans and the British as they competed to gain control over it. Qatar is a desert with few highlands. Its weather is very hot and humid with very little rain. Its population turned to the sea for their livelihood. Most of the income was coming from pear hunting, processing, and exporting. Fish was the second activity of people.

Qatar has been a tribal society. It was nomadic in the eighteenth century. Tribal tradition and nomadic institutions governed their lives. Gradually Islamic jurisprudence began to replace most of the tribal tradition. Sheikh Jassim and his father had their great role in this process as well as the unifying of the tribes. The society of Qatar became a group, fighting together when it was necessary regardless of their tribal belonging.

Sheikh Jassim was known to have a comprehensive look, which went to the entire region of the Arab Gulf and Arabian Peninsula. He thought that security and stability of the region was as important as his own entity. That was the reason we saw him in the center of events even though they were outside Qatar. He was in full agreement and cooperation with Sultan Abdul Hameed to the extent that all the false accusations and gossip of Sheikh Jassim's enemies were rejected by the sultan but were turned in favor of him. The climax of the position of Sheikh Jassim was when Nafith Pasha, the governor of Basra, recommended Sheikh Jassim for the highest medal of honor, which was approved immediately by the Sultan. Moreover, when another governor of Basra made a false accusation about Sheikh Jassim and attacked Qatar, the sultan fired the governor and declared Sheikh Jassim district administrator of Qatar.

Sheikh Jassim had to go through a difficult struggle with the British as they attempted to take over Qatar by war or through protection. The British resident in Bahrain visited Sheikh Jassim, who refused to meet him on a British ship but in Sheikh Jassim's palace. On the other hand, when he expelled the Indian Banyans from Qatar, the British objected strongly and demanded compensation. Sheikh Jassim thought he could either pay them or enter in a war, which the British would win. He paid the compensations.

We discussed Midhat Pasha's campaign in detail because it affected the region security and stability; it was an opportunity for the Ottomans to show their strength and control of the region and give a lesson to the rebellion that took over Al-Ahsa'a and other territories with help from the British. However, the campaign was an exaggeration in its manpower, weapons, and involvement of several entities of the region. Sheikh Jassim was smart enough to invite the campaign to Qatar instead of letting the troops enter Qatar by war as it did in other entities.

The Midhat Pasha campaign was successful in accomplishing all its goals we stated above. Though it came after a long slumber, it was thought by people of the Arab Gulf and Arabian Peninsula as an awakening call of the Ottoman Empire. However, the government and its subordinates, military and civilian, went back to sleep again, allowing its officials to receive bribes and overtaxing people for themselves, etc. Hence, the campaign lost all its accomplishments within a short period.

SHEIKH JASSIM BIN THANI

I thought the best person who could give a description of Sheikh Jassim is one of his descendants, Sheikh Khalid bin Mohammed bin Ghanim Al-Thani. Sheikh Khalid was born in Doha, Qatar, in 1983. He received his master's degree in Islamic Jurisprudence. He is considered an historian and writer. He wrote an article, "Views on Some Parts of the Life of Sheikh Jassim," published in the Qatari journal *The Arabs*, from which we shall cite some excerpts:

> In the Name of Allah the most Gracious most Merciful. Praise be to Allah the Lord of the worlds, peace be upon Mohammed and his family and companions.
>
> These are general views on the life of the founder of Qatar Sheikh Jassim may Allah has his mercy on him. We have pointed at some of his wisdoms and lessons. They will guide you to the man and how he was of truthful, pious and dependent on Allah together with bravery and determination. We shall start with his name; he was Sheikh Jassim bin Mohammed bin Thani bin Mohammed . . . bin Mi'dhad . . . Bin Tamim . . . Adnan . . . Bin Prophet Ismael bin Prophet Ibrahim peace is upon them. That is why he was called Al-Mi'dhdi Al-Wahbi Al-Tuhri Al-Hendhali Al-Timimi. Since these were the renowned personalities in the line of his ancestry.

He was born in the year 1827 in the Muharaq Island of Bahrain. His mother was the female Sheikh Noora the daughter of Fahd Al-Kowari. He was raised by his father on the virtues of Islam and the best manners. He showed at early age signs of bravery, good characters and leadership.

Qatar, before Sheikh Jassim leadership was land of internal and external contrivances and disputes until Sheikh Jassim was able to unify its internal front. All people of Qatar rallied around him. They stood fast under his leadership against any foreign invader. He used his sharp mind to move his country through the struggle of world powers until he achieved his goal of independence.

Among his early stands that showed his bravery and knighthood was during the battle of Musaimer when he was 25 year old. He led the Qatari side of the battle. He challenged one of the leaders of the aggressor leaders and killed him. He mentioned the battle in his poem.

Another stand of him was in 1870. Some of Al-Wakeel's followers transgressed on a caravan of Al-Na'eem family and captured one of Al-Na'eem sheikhs. The Al-Na'eem family went to Sheikh Jassim in Doha asking for help. He agreed to help them providing that they were truthful and unified. He ordered to raise his flag outside Doha and have everybody join him. All people of Doha went out declaring readiness to fight with him. He led his people to the Wekra. When they reached it, the Wakeel's people freed the captured Sheikh and returned the things they took.

Another stand of him that indicated his adherence to Islam and his political wisdom was asking the Ottomans to send a military protective brigade to Qatar in 1871. He raised the Ottoman flag on his palace. He was granted the title of District Administrator of Qatar in 1876. He was in full in charge of his country. His invitation of the Ottomans to come to his country was an alternative of them going there in war. He wanted to close the door in the face of the British who were attempting to take over Qatar as they did with Bahrain and other areas.

Finally, when the Ottomans tried to establish a custom office in 1887 to show their authority in Qatar, he and his people refused that. Hence, in 1893 the tension reached its climax, when the Governor Mohammed Hafidh Pasha came to Qatar with an army to capture Sheikh Jassim. The Wejba Battle took place when Sheikh Jassim and his people were victorious.

All these stands indicate that Sheikh Jassim did not want injustice for his people. Even to impose custom duties on the merchants or their ships or taxes on pearl income were not acceptable because it would lead to their migration to another entity. He considered money that was levied from custom duties or other taxes were prohibited. Although he had to fight Ottoman troops in the Wejba battle because of the taxes, he did not pull his hands from it. He showed Sultan Abdul Hameed that the war was not his fault. The Sultan fired the Governor who started the battle.

Among his support of the Islamic nation was his support to Libyan liberation fighters against the Italians by sending them 20,000 Rupees. He also stood with Saudi Government and its founder King Abdul Aziz by sending money and weapon. He also sent a telegram to the Caliph explaining the case of the King. He sponsored writers to explain the Saudi case in the newspapers. These stands showed his following the news about the Islamic Nation regardless how far from Qatar they were.

He was known to welcome those who came to him when they were suppressed. He received Imam Abdul Rahman bin Faisal Al-Saud and his family including later King Abdul Aziz. Sheikh Jassim ordered his family to leave their living quarters for the guests. They stayed in Qatar several months before they went to Kuwait.

He also tried to release Sheikh Mohammed bin Khalifa who was imprisoned by the British to Eden to replace him by his son. Sheikh Jassim saw the imprisoned Sheikh in a dream as he mentioned that in one of his poems. He offered for his release 1,000 of his best camels and 90 of the best horses, but his intersession was refused. He also was among those who strived to release Al-Bassam family who was residing in Anza. King Abdul Aziz moved them to Riyadh for something they did. They stayed 15 months under restriction. Some dignitaries from Basra tried to intercede with great ransom but were rejected. Sheikh Jassim interceded for them. His intercession was accepted by the King and sent them with his servants to Qatar. Sheikh Jassim welcomed them generously. Sheikh Abdullah Al-Bassam mentioned that when they finished supper, his uncle Abdullah bin Abdul Rahman was washing his hands. His sight was very weak. He did not know that Sheikh Jassim was pouring the water for him. When his guide told him, he pulled his hands. Then Sheikh Jassim told him that I have 60 servants could do the job but I wanted to have the honor of serving you. After this incidence the Al-Bassam family was nicked name the liberated of Al-Thani.

He mentioned several other dignitaries who were imprisoned or restricted residency released with the intercession of Sheikh Jassim. He also set the paste for his son and his descendants after that to intercede for those needed help. Now we see hundreds of people who were kicked out of their countries were welcomed in Qatar because they were unjustly treated in their homeland. Sheikh Jassim wrote long poem showing his conduct of helping oppressed people for his descendants to follow.

Sheikh Jassim was very religious not in the sense of performing prayers, fasting, giving zakat and making pilgrimage only, but also Islam was his way of life. He used to give sermons every Friday, give lessons after prayers; spent lot of money on religious schools and ruled according to the Islamic jurisprudence. He included his adherence to religion and ruled with it in many of his poems and his will. He also spent great deal of money to encourage students of religion and their teachers. He dedicated properties as endowments for schools and mosques not only in Qatar but also in many other countries. He sent many students to other countries from his money to study in order to return home to teach others.

Sheikh Jassim was concerned in printing books to be distributed freely. He used to select good books to be reprinted in India without mentioning his name. His successors followed suit in reprinting books to be distributed to students.

Sheikh Jassim had two families; his immediate family that consisted of his parents, wives, sons, brothers and his other relatives. The other family was his people of Qatar who loved him and he loved them dearly. Hence, he was sincere with them and they followed him and supported him.

His all year round business, political involvement and administrative duties did not keep him away of caring for his family. He loved them and cared for them. When his wife Noor bint Mohammed Al-Ghanim who was the mother of his three children; Ali, Abdullah and Ghanim died he wrote two long elegiac poetry. He included his sadness of losing her, his acceptance of Allah's predetermine and his patience.

Francis Bride, the British Political Agent in Bahrain described his visit to Sheikh Jassim in his farm 1905 by saying, "I was surprised to see such beautiful garden well organized surrounded by tamarisk trees with clover grass between them. There were many pomegranate trees and about 300 palm trees. There was a sitting place that had full view of the garden. I saw a well respectable man sitting there with a six year old child in his lap. Sheikh Jassim had beard with white hair, but he looked much younger than his age. Although he was known to have strong and tough personality, he was lovable generous man. He welcomed me very well. From our conversation, I noticed that he was very knowledgeable about politics and world affairs. He kept repeating, however, that he is retiring from these matters."

Among his wise decisions, he spread his sons in different areas and away from his residence. He constructed those areas where his sons lived under their supervision. Besides, there were two other advantages for such decision; they would be safer and could control the entire country. He cared very much for his other relatives. He granted them palaces and provided them with what they need.

Sheikh Jassim was quite versed in poetry. He made plentiful poems in practically all subjects. Most his poetry was colloquial, which strongly affected people at that time.
He was praised by many contemporary poets and by those who came later.

Sheikh Jassim died Friday July 17, 1913. Many poets and writers bemoaning him show that his departure was a great loss for the Muslim nation. However, his tradition, his will, his poems and the way he raised his sons had great impact on his successors and their administrative and policy system.

* * *

SOURCES AND REFERENCES

Documents

HR SYS 108, 5 (1893, 22–04), 4.

HR SYS 114, 35 (1893, 22, 04), 12.

Y. MTV 231, 120 (1320, Ra 19), 1.

YA Res. 90, 30, (1315, B10), 2.

BOS, YEE 14/2 50/12 6/8–5.

BOA, MHMd 111, p. 719.

BOA, MHMd 71, p. 353.

BOA, YEE 14/2256/126/11, S. 5.

BOA, YEE 14/2256/126/17, p. 5.

BOA, YEE 14/255/126/8, 21-8-1313H, p. 2.

BOA, YEE 18/553 – 141.93.94.

BOA, YEE 14/366/ 126/9, p. 1–2.

HE 20525 1255.

BOA, YA Hus. 272/95.

BOA, YEE 14/2 50//12 6/8.

BOA, YA Res. 90/25, 30.

BOA, YA Res. 90/30.

BOA, YA Res. 91/29.

BOA, YEE 36/139–69/139/XVIII.

BOA, YA Res. 93/21.

BOS, YA Res. 94/10.

Oztuna, Yilmaz. 1965. *Turkiye Tarihi*. Istanbul.

Arsiv Belgeleri Isigi altinda Katar'da Osmali Hakimiyeti/Osman Zeki Soyyigit (PhD thesis) 1990. Istanbul.

Classification of decree, Special Council: 1611.

Classification of decree, Special Council: 1624.

Classification of decree, Internal Decree: 43194.

Classification of decree, Special Council: 1667, 1, 3, 9.

BOA, Agreement Text, 17/242.

Classification of decree, Internal Decree: 83926.

Classification of decree, Internal Decree: 44002.

Classification of decree, Internal Decree: 44196.

Classification of decree, Internal Decree: 44230.

Classification of decree, Internal Decree: 44822.

Classification of decree, Internal Decree: 44930.

Classification of decree, Special Council: 4699.

Classification of decree, Military Decree: 27 May. 1310/16.

Directorate of files archive, supreme decrees, document #1310/M/16, dated 24/1/1310.

Classification of decree, Military Decree: 27 May. 1310/16.

Ottoman Archive, classification decree, IDAH 44930, cited from Dr. Suhail Saban, National King Fahd Library Press, Riyadh 2005.

BOOKS

Bayat, Fadhil. 2010. *Arabian Nations*. The Ottoman Archive, Research Center for Islamic History, Arts and Culture. Istanbul.

Sa'dawi, Salih, translator. 2008. Research Center for Islamic History, Arts and Culture. Istanbul.

Al-Shuraifi, Ibrahim bin Dikhneh. 1999. *Al-Ma'adhid and Qatar*. Kuwait.

Al-Ben'ali, Rashid bin Fadhil. 2007. *Majmoo' Alfadha'il fe fen Alneseb we Tareekh Alqaba'il*, second printing. Doha: Bedr Publishing.

Korshon, Zechariah. 2005. "Nejd Coast: Al-Ahsa'a" in the Ottoman Archive. Beirut: Arabian House for Encyclopedia.

Ibid. 2008. *Qatar during the Ottoman Era*. Beirut: Arabian House for Encyclopedia.

Herman Burkhart: "A Voyage cross the Arab Gulf" written by Niba and Herbestroit, translated by Dr. Ahmad Eibish, (Abu Dhabi: Cultural Center, 2009)

Al-Dakheel, Suleiman bin Salih. 1931. *Tuhfat Alalibba' in the History of Al-Ahsa'a*. Baghdad: Riyadh Press.

Al-Sheikh, Dr. Abdul Rahman Abdullah, trans. Complete Records of Alfonse Delbukerk. Abu Dhabi: Cultural Center.

Ibn A'sakir, Rashid bin Mohammed. Religious endowments and charitable works of Sheikh Jassim bin Mohammed Al-Thani, the Amir of Qatar, handwritten pamphlet. Riyadh: 1429 H.

Alazhar alnaddeh min ash'aar albadieh, fifth printing. Al-Ta'if: Al-Ma'arif Library 1420 H.

Diwan Sheikh Qassim bin Mohammed Al-Thani (Doha 1423 H)

Al-Zerkely, Khairiddin bin Mahmoud, Al-A'alam

Al-Rihani, Ameen. 1928. *History of Nejd and Subjoined Areas*. Beirut: Yusuf Scientific Press.

Ibid. *Arabia Kings*, two volumes. Beirut: Dar Al-Jeel.

"Gulf tribes" in Lorimar's bibliography. 2003. Qatar: Dar Althqafa.

Arabic Language Journal, third year, vol. 5. 1913.

Ibn Al-Iraq, Sheikh Nu'man bin Mohammed. Ma'din Aljawahir fi Tareekh Al-Basra wa al-jazza'ir.

Qatari Arab Newspaper, number 7494, December 18, 2008.

REFERENCES:

Ibn Mendhoor. 2008. Lisan Al-Arab. Beirut: Dar Sadir.

Ibn Al-Ghimlass. 2008. Al-Basra, wla'eha wa mutesalimouha. Beirut: Dar Al-Arabia lilmouso'at

Al-Bairouni, Aljamahir fi Ma'arifet Aljawahir. (No publisher or date.)

Al-Jeberti, Sheikh Abdul Rahman. 2007. Summary of Al-Jeberti History. Cairo: Dar of Scientific Books Publication.

Al-Hamdani, Dr. Tariq Nafi'. 2010. Historical News of Arab Gulf in the Newspapers of *Arab Language* and *Indian Arabs*. London: Al-Warraq for Publication.

Al-Haidari Al-Baghdadi, Ibrahim bin Asa'ad. 1999. E'nwan Almajd fi Bayan Ahwal Baghdad, Basra and Nejd. Beirut: Dar Al-Arabia Lilmouso'at.

Al-Khalifa, May Mohammed. 1999. Al-Istora wa Altarikh Almwazi. Beirut: Arabian Institute for Studies and Publications.

Al-Uthaimeen, Dr. Abdullah Salih. 2009. *History of Saudi Arabia*, vol. 1, 15th printing Riyadh: Alobaican Library.

Al-Shalaq, Dr. Ahmad et al. 2006. *Political Development of Qatar from an Emirate to its Independence*. Doha: Renod Modern Press.

Al-Shibani, Mohammed Sharif. 1963. *Arabian Qatar Emirate, between the Past and Present*. Beirut: Dar Althaqafa.

Al-A'abid, Dr. Fo'ad Sa'eed. 1984. *British Policy in the Arab Gulf 1853–1914*. Kuwait: That Alsalasil.

Al-I'ryan, Dr. Munira Abdullah. 1990. The Relations between Nejd and the Surrounding Powers. Kuwait That Alsalasil.

Ra'ees, George. 2003. *Oman and the Southern Coast of the Gulf.* Cairo: Cultural Religion Library.

Ramadan, Dr. Mahmoud. 2006. *Qatar in the Geographic and Historical Maps.* Cairo: Center of Arabian Culture.

Shubber, Majid. 2010. *The Tribes and Political and Tribal Struggle in the Reports of the Officers and British Envoys during the 18th and 19th Centuries.* London: Dar Alwarraq for Publication.

Tehboob, Dr. Fa'iq Hamdi. 1983. *Bahrain Political History.* Kuwait: That alsalasil.

Korshon, Zechariah. 2010. *The Ottomans and Aal Saud in the Ottoman Archive, 1745–1914.* Beirut: Dar Al-Arabia of Encyclopedia.

Lorimar. *Guidebook of the Gulf,* Historical Section, vol. 1.

Abdul Rahim, Abdul Rahman. 1983. *From the Documents of the First Saudi State during Mohammed Ali Era.* Cairo: Dar Alkitab Aljami'I.

Qassim, Jamal Zachariah. *Arab Gulf Book.* Beirut: Dar Alfikr Alarabi.

Nekhleh, Dr. Mohammed Arabi. 1980. *Al-Ahsa'a Political History, 1818–1913.* Kuwait: Dar Alsalasil.

* * *

ENDNOTES

(ENDNOTES)

CHAPTER 1

[1]   Mohammed Ali Pasha was born in Quola in the northern part of Greece in 1769. The information about him is very scarce, except that he was an orphan raised by his father's friend Ismael Al-Shourbachi. He was anti-Islam and Muslims. He was working against the Ottoman Empire secretly in plots and conspiracies. His alliance was with the French. He sent the Egyptian army to Syria on the way to attack Istanbul. He conspired with Shah Iran to let the latter take over Baghdad, while his warships reached Basra. During his reign in Egypt, he forbade the calling for the Islamic prayers and encouraged alcoholic consumption and other anti-Islamic practices. With all that he was doing, the Ottoman sultan did not stand firmly against such unknown wickedness. Last but not least, his sons led a campaign attacking the two Holy Cities, killing innocent people, destroying properties, and confiscating what they could carry to Egypt.

[2]   Ibn Khaldoun is Wallieddeen Abdul Rahman bin Mohammed . . . Al-Hathrami. He was born in Tunis in 1332 and died in 1406. He is known to be the founder of sociology. His forefa-

thers received high political and religious posts in Andalusia. Historians related several publications in history, mathematics, and logics. He was well known with his famous book *Alkhabar fi Diwan Almubtada'a WA Alkhabar fi Ayyam Alarab WA Al'ajam WA Albarbar WA men A'assarahum men AL Sultan Alakbar.* The book is in seven volumes; the first was the renowned "Al-Muqadima" (the Introduction). In the Muqadima, Ibn Khaldoun gives a summary of all that he wrote in the book of all sciences and subjects: geography, urbanization, astronomy, sociology, social relations, human behavior, etc. He and his accomplishments were highly recognized by great men like Toyimbi, Maxim Gorki, Lenin, etc.

3   Suleiman bin Salih Al-Dakheel Al-Nejdi. He was a contemporary to Sheikh Jassim. He wrote about Sheikh Jassim that he was among the great men of the Arabs. He was well respected and admired by his people and others in the Arab Gulf and Arabian Peninsula entities. Sheikh Jassim was able to bring together various tribesmen in an alliance through his effective personality. He led them to the establishment of independent Qatar. Hence the testimony of Suleiman, the well- known journalist and great person, is well taken.

4   Holy Quran, chapter 3, verse 102.

5   Holy Quran, chapter 59, verse 18.

6   Holy Quran, chapter 31, verses 33–34.

7   Prophet Mohammed saying, cited in Sahih Muslim.

8   Holy Quran, chapter 4, verse 116.

9   Holy Quran, chapter 51, verses 22, 23 and 56.

10   Holy Quran, chapter 63, verse 9.

CHAPTER 2

11   The Arab Gulf is a water extension of the Arab Sea. It is between the Gulf of Oman and Shatt-el-Arab River. Its western shores

are the Arabian Peninsula, and the eastern shores are currently belonging to Iran after the shah of Iran took it over from the Arabian tribes who resided there for several centuries. The total area of the Arab Gulf is 233,100 km. Its width is between 55 km and 370 km in the north. It is relatively shallow. Its deepest point is about 90 meters, which makes it easier to reach the bottom for pearl hunting. The Arab Gulf has more than 130 islands, the largest of which are Qasham, Bobian, and the Bahraini Islands. The Gulf is very hot during the summer, and its winter is relatively cold. Such changes in the temperature create seasonal migration of its fish.

12 Sheikh Mohammed bin Abdul Wahhab is descended from Bani Tamim, the greatest Arabian tribe. He is not a sheikh of the tribe but a religious authority, known as a reformer. He was born in a village north of Riyadh in 1703. He died in the same village in 1791. After learning Islamic knowledge in Mecca and Medina from renowned scholars, he returned to his area to find people had gone astray from the original religion of Islam. He began with his relatives and people of his area, teaching them the right religion. He gradually gained followers to spread his ideas of rejecting innovation and invention in religion as well as getting rid of the associating partners with Allah by requesting from the dead whoever they are. He also fought against those who deviated from religion by committing unlawful acts such as stealing, fornication, alcoholic consumption, etc. His ideas are the bases of the sect followed in Saudi Arabia today.

13 Maria Teresa Rial is a silver coin initiated in France and Austria. It has the photo of the Empress and in the back the Habsburg emblem of the eagle of two heads. It was used intensively in the Arab Gulf, the Arabian Peninsula, Yemen, and East and North Africa. The demand for this coin continued even after the death of the empress. That is why they continued to make it with the same 1780 date for about two centuries.

Chapter 3

14   He is Bari Muhieddeen, a geographer and a sea amir (1465–1554). He participated in saving Muslims of Andalusia from the massacres of hundreds of thousands by the Christians and Jews of Spain. He and his uncle Kamal moved as many as possible to North Africa. He drew the world map from his travelling. He also wrote a book, *The Book of Maritime*. He was appointed the maritime commander of Egypt after being taken over by Sultan Yawez. He was hanged as being accused of taking booties for himself while he was taking them to Egypt to be sent to Istanbul.

15   He was the greatest Safavids king. He was a seventeen-year-old when he overthrew his father to rule for forty-two years. He was a fanatical bloody Shi'a. The Safavids were Aatherians but not Persians. They were Sunni Sufis but changed to Shi'a. At the beginning of his rule, he made a peaceful agreement with the Ottomans because he was unable to fight them. When he became strong, he attacked the Ottomans to take over Iraq. He made the greatest massacres in the Sunnis and destroyed their sheikhs' tombs. He offered his alliance and full cooperation to the British to destroy the Ottomans. He tried to convince the Iranians to stop going to Mecca for a pilgrimage and replace that with visiting the tomb of Ali bin Musa Al-Ridha in Meshhad because Mecca is controlled by the Sunnis.

16   It was established by a decree from the British Queen Elizabeth the First on December 31, 1600. It was granted a monopoly of trade in India and other British colonies in the East. It was given more authorities to undertake all economic activities in the British colonies with great political influence. Later on, it extended its activities to the Arab Gulf area. It continued until 1858.

17   Al-Ahwaz is a natural and geographic extension of Mesopotamia. After it was captured by the Islamic troops led by Abu Musa Al-Ash'ari in 637, it remained under the Islamic rule as part of the Basra governorate until 1258 during the Mongolian

invasion. During the period 1436–1724, it became under the rule of the Musha'sh'ia Arabian State. Both the Ottoman and Safavids governments recognized its independence. It was ruled after that by the Arabian Ka'bi tribe (1724–1925). The British tricked its amir, Sheikh Khaz'al, by inviting him to their ship, and they captured him. They attacked his emirate and gave it to their ally, the Persians, as part of some political arrangements between the two governments. It should be noted that the people of Al-Ahwaz never stopped fighting for their independence from the British in spite of being replaced by Iranians and following ethnic cleansing.

Chapter 5

18 This decision was taken after the review of the situation by Midhat Pasha in light of the secret report of the envoy sent on the ship. The report showed the existence of the British in Bahrain. The decision also showed the instructions of Midhat Pasha and his deep relations with the British.

19 The meant to appoint Sheikh Abdullah Al-Faisal as an Ottoman employee. His authority, which would go beyond Nejd, derived from the Ottoman government, just like what happened with Sheikh of Al-Muntifiq.

20 This is another stumble of the Ottomans who showed that they would not do anything as their responsibility toward the territories they occupied or considered themselves as the protectors of the Muslims as they claimed. It sounded ridiculous to liberate one of their territories at the expense of someone else, regardless of his involvement.

Chapter 7

21 Sultan Abdul Hameed the Second was born in 1842. He became the caliph in 1876 until he was removed by a coup in

1909. He accompanied his uncle, Sultan Abdul Aziz, in 1867 to meet Napoleon the third, British Queen Victoria, King of Belgium, King of Prussia, the German czar, et al. He received them in Istanbul later. He was very smart, brave, and had depth in understanding what was going on in the world. He was very religious, not only in performing prayers and other duties but also in his decision making. His reign was a surprise to all those groups and governments that were conspiring to get rid of the Islamic rule such as the British, Europeans, Masonic societies, and Jewish organizations. All these worked very hard to create secular groups of Turkish intellectuals. At the beginning of his rule, he appointed Midhat Pasha as his prime minister. He gave into the pressure of having a constitution and general election. He said his famous statement, "If you are among wolves, you have to howl like them". He was able to fire Midhat Pasha, the enemy of the caliphate, and the accused of killing his uncle Sultan Abdul Aziz. He put him on trial according to the constitution that Midhat Pasha was most an advocate. The latter was imprisoned accordingly. He recognized those high officials for their briberies. He tried his utmost to prevent the British from dominating the Muslim lands. But he seemed to be running against a strong draft by himself. After he was overthrown, he was exiled to Salaneek to be returned to Istanbul where he died in 1918.

ABOUT THE AUTHOR

Omar AL-EJLI

"Omar AL-EJLI is an Iraqi scholar and historian. He was born in Baghdad, 1953. He received his BA (Economics) from Basrah University, 1976 and his MA (Economics) from Basrah University too. He got his PhD from the Arab History Institute for Higher Studies, Baghdad, 1997.

He has established Nahawand Center in Singapore. The Center is mainly concerned with studying the Ottoman Archive from which several studies were published. Based on his work, two critically-acclaimed TV series were created. He has published three books in Arabic; "Economic System of the Abbasside Dynasty", "Sheikh Jassim Al-Thani: Founder of Qatar" and "Sultanate Oman: Economic and historical conditions". He wrote several articles in renowned journals in history, economics, culture and religion. He is a member of:
- The Arab Historian Union.
- Human Rights & International Organization For Developments.
- The Arab Union for the Protection of intellectual rights.
and the Japanese Society for Cultural Dialogue. He is fluent in Arabic, English and Esperanto. AL-EJLI is currently residing with his family in Doha, Qatar."

CPSIA information can be obtained at www.ICGtesting.com
Printed in the USA
LVOW09s0428180116

470924LV00003B/7/P